Snowed in with Ski Patrol

A SECOND CHANCE WINTER ROMANCE

RACHEL KAYE

BOOK & BREW CREATIVE LLC

For Michelle.

I hope heaven is a field of lavender.

I hope it is a dirty martini—but only the kind with blue cheese stuffed olives.

I hope it is an endless row of dogs lining up for you to give them love.

I hope it is perfect peace.

Content Note

Snowed in with Ski Patrol is part of *The Holly Hill Winter Novella Collection*, a complete series of interconnected stand-alone romance novellas set in the fictional small town of Holly Hill. Each novella can be read in any order. If you read all three, you may catch glimpses of familiar characters.

This book is an open-door romance featuring on-page sexual content.

There may be topics in *Snowed in with Ski Patrol* that lead to discomfort. Please treat yourself kindly.

-Frank discussion of parental death. The death is depicted on page.

-On page depiction of grief response and character's participation in grief support group.

-On page discussion of Post-traumatic Stress Disorder and associated coping responses.

-Brief mention of a side character who experienced a Traumatic Brain Injury. Not depicted on page.

-Intense sipping...you've been warned.

welcome to HOLLY HILL

SNOWCAP CAFE

219

MAIN STREET

HOLLY PEAK HWY

Holly Peak

the cabin

CHAPTER ONE

Wren

THE COFFEE SHOP—CALLED SNOWCAP Café—is cozy, like a log cabin nestled in a copse of trees, hidden in the most insulated part of the forest. The surrounding town of Holly Hill is equally cute, crackling with that early winter feeling, the one that pre-dates holiday burnout and the February doldrums.

I hate it, but I need to be here to finish what I started.

The wide-eyed barista behind the counter tucks a stray bit of hair behind her ear as she casts me a nervous grin. There is a tiny brown stain marring her otherwise adorable sweater. I fight to tame a scowl, though I'm positive I look about as friendly as an alley cat right now.

"Welcome to Snowcap!" her voice rings through the air. It reminds me of a Christmas song or one of those local TV commercial jingles.

Blegh.

"Do you need a minute to look at the menu?" she trills, looking at me expectantly.

"You tell me what I should get."

I'm not in the frame of mind to do any thinking right now—not today of all days. I need to grab some sustenance, get up the mountain, and forget about everything dragging me down.

I need to be weightless.

"We're best known for our dirty chai lattes and avocado toast. Would that work for you?"

I force my lips to tilt in an upward direction. "Sure." I steal a look at her name tag. "Thanks, Alice."

See, I do know how to be nice.

She rings me up, writing my name at the top of an order slip. The W curls over the top of the other words like the inverted arch of a ski.

"It'll be about five minutes."

I nod, reasoning that gives me enough time to run to my vehicle to grab my gear and change in the bathroom. The drive to Holly Peak is short. I can handle the feeling of bundled-up discomfort for the trip.

A sharp blast of wind cuts through my puffer coat as I jog to the side street where I parked. I make quick work of grabbing my backpack from the overfilled rear hatch. The streets are eerily empty as I make my way back inside the cloying warmth that is Snowcap.

I follow a trail of artwork and colorful tapestries to find the bathroom tucked away in a nook behind the fireplace. I can hear a man with a gruff voice yelling through the door.

I wait a beat, listening for an answering voice, maybe a scream or a whimper. There are a few seconds of silence before the man starts in again, clearly on the phone with someone he isn't happy with.

Rude. Who takes a phone call in a public bathroom when there are other people who might need to use it?

I look at my beat-up sports watch, noting that there is still time before Holly Peak closes. But if I don't change soon, I won't make it up the mountain in time.

I wait a few minutes, but soon enough, I hear the barista—Alice—call my name in the sing-song voice that is weirdly growing on me. I hustle back down the hallway, my bag slipping precariously from my shoulder and throwing me off balance.

"One dirty chai and avocado toast for the lady," Alice says, sliding me a porcelain plate with a ring of cerulean flowers around the inner edge. It's so cute and delicate that I'm tempted to launch it toward the stonework on the fireplace. Somehow, I doubt Alice would appreciate my shattering her precious dishware.

The spices in the chai tickle my nose as I pull up a chair at one of the reclaimed wood tables. I'd love to savor the flavors, but unfortunately, a swift chug is in my future.

I swirl the liquid in the mug as I rip off bites of avocado toast with my teeth. I tuck my bag securely between my jiggling legs, not caring that my ski pants are hanging out halfway. I'm sure I look like a ball of nervous energy to anyone observing.

The truth is, I am nervous, though I'm loath to admit it.

I don't want to be at this café. I don't want to be in Holly Hill. And most of all, I don't want to be around other people. All I want to do is get back on the slopes.

My phone vibrates ominously along the table. Swiping my crummy fingers along my black leggings, I pick it up to look at the screen.

Travel advisory issued for the following counties...

There are several unfamiliar ones listed, but I recognize the county that Holly Hill sits in.

Yet another reason for me to get where I'm going—and fast.

From where I'm sitting, I'm still close enough to hear that dickhead having a tantrum in the bathroom. I shove back from my seat, taking the last swig of my latte as I walk toward the counter.

"Done already?" Alice asks.

"Yep. Do you have a room where I can change?"

Her eyes widen a fraction, but to her credit, she rolls with the punches and doesn't ask questions.

"You can sneak into the break room if you want."

I duck past her, behind the counter, and into the small, cluttered room she directs me toward. It doesn't take me long to change, slipping into the familiar layers of clothing.

Alice gives me a startled look when I reappear. "Those pants are...interesting," she says, one delicate feathered eyebrow shooting sky-high.

It would be more accurate to call the pants obnoxious. They're a riotous swirl of colors—all purple and neon green, magenta and orange.

They are hideous and unflattering and the most sentimental item of clothing I own. I'll never get rid of them.

"I like abstract art," I reply. My voice is strange and out of practice.

"Skiing?"

"Yep."

"Be careful out there. A storm is rolling in any minute."

"Shockingly, people who ski tend to like snow."

Even her chortling laugh somehow sounds melodic. "I knew my grumpiest customer had a sense of humor lurking under there somewhere!"

There is no way I'm her grumpiest customer, not when that dude in the bathroom is probably still carrying on.

Her smile is eager, like she's waiting for my laugh to harmonize with hers.

"I gotta go," I say, pushing past her and the dwindling crowd in the café. The door is five steps away and my car not much farther than that.

"Wren!" Alice's cheerful voice cuts through the ambient chatter and whirring coffee grinders. "I mean it. Be careful out there!"

I never am, but that's the point.

🫘 🫘 🫘 🫘 🫘 🫘 🫘

HOLLY PEAK IS LESS a mountain and more a very, very steep hill. The mountains in this area are so ancient they're shrinking. Some people think they're less fun, not so extreme, but Dad loved this part of the country.

I garnered a few strange looks when I checked in at the resort, everyone else fumbling to reach their minivans and hatchbacks before the worst of the snow hit. I lied and said I was going to my rented room, only veering toward the trails once I turned a corner. It was a wonder no one noticed me hauling my skis with me.

I stare down the trail, taking a bracing breath. I didn't bother with the ski lift, what with my trying to be as incognito as possible. I've invested, in recent months, in special removable inserts for my boot bindings—ones that allow my heel free range of movement for the trek up the mountain. Even my skis have specialized fabric skins to make climbing uphill easier.

Holly Peak isn't steep. It didn't take me long to hike to the top of the trail denoted by a blue square. It will be an even faster ride down. Dad would have given me crap for taking the easier run, but I'm too tired for a double-black today.

I fumble with my ski pole as I dig into the interior pocket of my jacket, searching for the plastic bag I put there this morning. The last bag. Tugging a thick glove off with my teeth, I slide the zipper of the bag gingerly as a blast of icy wind nearly causes me to spill its contents entirely. My body is wracked by an involuntary shiver. I need to get this over with before the snowstorm derails my plans.

Shifting on my feet, I push off my skis. I'm not as out of practice as I was when I started skiing again last February. My legs aren't quite as wobbly, and my breath doesn't catch in my throat anymore.

I shake my head from side to side as I descend, tipping the plastic bag upside down as I glide. The motion has me slightly off balance, but I won't abandon my sole reason for being here.

I leap into the air with an experimental, playful move. I love this feeling more than anything else in the world. The weightless exhilaration. The rolling sensation, like riding atop a frozen wave. The pinch of cold air in my lungs when I fill them almost to bursting.

The landing is jarring. Dad would have been embarrassed; I was smoother when I was nineteen. Another gust of wind catches the plastic bag.

My fingers, clumsy in my thick gloves, fumble with the thin, slippery material. The bag is nearly empty, my task so close to completion. Losing it now is not an option.

I clutch the bag tightly in my fist, breathing a sigh of relief as I secure it between clenched fingers.

I'm so focused on the item in my hand that I almost miss the tree. I twist rapidly, but my reaction time is a split second too slow. Though my body doesn't make contact, the back edge of my ski smacks against the thick trunk. The resulting scrape reverberates through my teeth. My ski poles drag in the snow as I work to keep myself upright.

It's futile, and I feel myself tilting headfirst. Both ski poles fly, and I'm certain the trail is reminiscent of our front lawn that one summer Dad gave away all his old fishing gear in a yard sale—things scattered everywhere. By some feat of long-dormant athleticism, I come down on my hip instead, but one foot is twisted awkwardly.

"Fuck!" I yell, the word flying away on the wind.

Chapter Two

Wren

I slam my hands on the snow when my third attempt at getting back on my feet fails. I've tried standing while clicked into my skis, and with the bindings released. Neither made a difference. Something happened to my ankle when I fell. A sprain, maybe. God forbid it's a break, and I have to seek medical attention.

But I have to do something, I realize. I'm apathetic, but I don't have a death wish.

Not really.

I reach into the pocket of my ski pants, searching for my cell phone. If I don't have service, I'm royally fucked.

I get lucky when the Holly Peak app loads, the number for ski patrol dispatch flashing on a yellow banner on the top half of the screen. I groan, then reluctantly dial the numbers.

"Holly Peak dispatch. What is your emergency?"

I fill the dispatcher in on my injury before sharing my place on the map. Her heavy sigh clues me in that no one is going to be thrilled about going out in this weather, especially when I bypassed safety protocols to come out here.

"I'll get someone to your location shortly."

The call ends more abruptly than I expect. A quick glance shows me that my phone is dead. My streak of luck is over already.

Are you proud of me, Dad? I think, huddling in on myself. These old pants of mine are no match for the wind as it howls down the trail. I don't dare risk trying to remove my boot to check on my ankle, lest I invite the cold in further.

I have no idea how long it will be before patrol arrives. It's a peculiar feeling, waiting for—anticipating—the arrival of ski patrol. Ten years ago, I'd be doing everything in my power to evade the so-called *Fun Police.*

Flopping back onto the powdery snow, I look up at the ominous sky. I can tell from the position of the barely visible sun that some time has passed, but I'm too tired to check my wristwatch. It isn't like it matters, anyway. Whoever dispatch sends will either get to me, or they won't.

It's ironic that this last task—the mission Dad didn't ask me to fulfill but I plan on doing anyway—just might be the end of me.

And who would even care? The other people in my virtual grief support group would notice, sure, but *care?* They'd just as soon figure I dropped out like so many others have in the months since we started meeting. It's been a slow trickle of attrition, something Marcqui, the counselor who facilitates the weekly meetings, warned us would happen.

The people who've left the group fit into three categories from what I've observed. There were those who attended one meeting and never returned. Others, like Mike and Joanne and Ahsan, were regulars, sharing their progress each week, their smiles looking less strained each time their faces popped up on the other end of my screen. They considered themselves healed enough that they didn't need the rest of us anymore.

Others just...withered away before they disappeared entirely.

I wonder what category they'll sort me into.

The inside of my ski goggles is suspiciously misty when I hear it—the heaving pants of some sort of animal. I push up into a seated position, blinking back into focus.

An enormous dog, white with patches of reddish-brown over each ear and along its body, cleaves its way through the snow, having the time of its life. The red vest with a white cross on the side identifies this dog for what it is: my knight in shining armor.

The dog slows as it comes to my side, nudging its great snout into my face. A glob of slobber hits the face of my goggles, and I laugh for the first time in forever.

"Hi, big guy," I whisper into the dog's fur.

I'm still laughing when the distinctive swish of skis reaches my ears.

It's a shame the dog isn't my sole rescuer. Dogs are so much easier than people.

"Hugo."

The dog jerks to attention, and all my senses go alert at the man's voice. It's deep and commanding—and strangely familiar—with a slight rasp that's notable, even muffled by the ski mask blocking the lower half of his face. The other half is hidden under blue-black reflective goggles topped with a matte-black helmet.

"Hugo," he says again, firmer this time. The dog—who looks *just* like a Hugo—shoves his cold, wet nose into my neck, finding the sliver of bare skin between my layers.

The patroller pulls to a halt, dragging a faded-red toboggan behind him. Hugo hops over, settling near the patroller's skis. I miss the comfort of the dog's touch. It's been a while since I let anyone—animal or human—get close, and it feels good.

I give my rescuer a surreptitious look, taking him in fully. He's motionless, his head tipped down toward my pant legs. I get the impression he's glaring, though I can't catch the barest hint of his face. He's cloaked in a cape of red nylon and white crosses. The anonymity should be alarming, but it isn't. Not even a little.

He lifts his helmeted head, catching me staring. I hold his gaze, unwilling to cave in to embarrassment. The wind stops, and it's completely silent as we look at each other. There is something about him that seems...

A rough static noise cuts in from the radio in his chest pocket, breaking the moment. Hugo lets out one whooping bark at the sound.

I must be going crazy, whether from grief or delirium or the nagging pain in my ankle. I don't know this ski patroller. I don't know anyone on this mountain, or in Holly Hill, or even in this part of the country.

He drops to a knee beside me and speaks to me for the first time. "I'm Nico. What's your name?"

That deep rasp sounds better than it did saying the dog's name. In my entire life, I've only ever felt tingles from one other man's voice. Now is not the time for those tingles to make a reappearance. Nico the Ski Patroller—who I can't even *see*—should not be inspiring lusty thoughts in me in the middle of a snowstorm.

But as inconvenient as the feeling is, I'm grateful to know I can still feel something for another person. It's been well over a year since I've felt anything even remotely close to attraction—and even longer since I've had sex.

I gasp when a warm hand—gloveless, rough, and slightly tanned—touches my left wrist.

"Checking your pulse," he says. "Can you speak?"

I nod, falling into the sound and the feel of him. I'm nervous, but I like it. He probably knows it too, given the fact that he's checking my heart rate.

His helmet shakes silently from side to side. I'm not sure if he's disapproving or if he finds me funny.

"Your name?" he prompts.

"Wren."

"What happened, Wren?"

"Uh, I fell. Got tangled up. I think I twisted my ankle. It doesn't feel too bad, though."

His fingers slip away from my wrist. I want to cry when he stows his hand back inside his thick, black glove.

"Take your goggles off."

"Huh?"

"Need to check your pupils."

"Oh, okay. But I didn't hit my head."

"I'm still gonna check."

I slip the goggles down until they dangle uselessly around my neck. The wind stings my eyes. I must have looked down without realizing, because Nico's hand is on my chin, tipping it up.

The only thing I see is my own face in the reflection of his goggles. I look as exhausted as I feel.

"Do you need to take your goggles off?" I ask, wondering how hard it is for him to complete his quick-and-dirty medical assessment in the middle of a snowstorm behind the screen of all those face coverings.

"Nope," he says before pulling back and rising up from his crouch.

Another loud shot of wind blows down the trail. The dog releases an anxious chuff. The storm has already picked up in the few minutes since Nico and Hugo arrived to pick me up.

"We need to go," Nico says. "Can you manage getting in the toboggan on your own?"

I eye the red metal sled. Skiing in these conditions is already going to be a challenge for Nico. Carting me down the trail is a greater burden.

It's humiliating. I used to laugh at the sad saps on the bunny hill who needed rescuing, determined never to be in their position.

It's Hugo who helps me power past my hesitation, nudging me with his nose toward the sled. Nico steadies his skis on the snow, standing downhill of the toboggan so it doesn't move as I scoot my way over the lip of the sled.

"Ready?" Nico asks once he's stowed my skis, his head aimed at me. I imagine a quirked brow under his goggles. I'm strangely incurious about his looks. He's competent and controlled in a way I can't help but appreciate. What he looks like beneath his layers doesn't change that for me.

"Ready," I reply with a nod, tucking my chin further into my collar.

Nico shoves off, and I simply watch as he maneuvers over the powder with grace, his movements a combination of small, rapid swings and wide, V-shaped motions that slow us down when needed. The toboggan is steady throughout. Hugo jogs alongside us, his great tongue flopping. I laugh, having more fun than someone caught in a snowstorm with a likely sprained ankle should be.

We turn down a narrow part of the trail, and I'm almost sad to catch sight of the castle-like resort building in the distance.

"What kind of dog is Hugo?" I ask during a lull in the whipping wind. I'm pretty sure I know, but I'm desperate to hear that raspy voice again. Desperate to keep some sort of human connection, even if it's with the man obligated to rescue me.

"Saint Bernard," he says, confirming my hunch.

"How long has he been with you?"

"Little over five years."

"Oh. Okay."

He doesn't want to talk, and that's fine. I wouldn't want to talk to me either. I got myself into a miserable mess, and he had to put himself and his dog at risk to dig me out.

I reach into my pocket, feeling for the small plastic bag inside. It's still there, though notably smaller than it was earlier. Even if Nico, with the sultry voice, doesn't want to indulge my weird aural fantasies, at least I've mostly accomplished what I set out to do. Dad would understand the reason for the delay.

"They're a good search-and-rescue breed."

I lift my head in surprise when Nico speaks again. Maybe he feels sorry for me or just wants to ease the awkwardness, but I don't mind. I'm *feeling* something with him again, even if our connection is destined to end when we reach the bottom of this trail.

"Some of the best avalanche dogs in history were the Saint Bernard breed," he continues. "Not as common nowadays, but this guy is special."

"Are there often avalanches out this way?"

It's a dumb question because I know the answer already, but it keeps Nico talking. I find that I like talking to him. It's natural, despite our tense situation. I don't mind talking to the other people in my support group, but that's structured—and *hard*. This is easy. It's like his grumpiness cancels out my sadness, and we're a hodge-podge of something new entirely.

"Nah. I got this guy when I lived in Wyoming. Worked out there briefly at one of the big resorts. Came here for a change of pace."

"I used to ski out West. Never Wyoming, though. Always wanted to get there." Ten years ago, I would have been riddled with the fear of missing out. Now I'm just glad to be slightly less numb than I was this morning.

"Yeah. I know."

"You know?"

A muffled cough comes from behind his face covering. "I know what you mean."

"Oh. Yeah. But you got there, right? That's pretty awesome."

The shoulders of his red jacket move in what I'm certain is a shrug. "Sometimes. Mostly it was lonely."

Loneliness: the most human of emotions. *That* I can relate to. Maybe that's the reason I feel this odd pull toward Nico, the reason he was the one to find me on this trail today. I reach for the bag in my pocket again, but before I can get there, the full, fluffy force of Hugo hits me like a truck as he throws his body into the toboggan.

"God damn it, Hugo!" Nico slides to a stop, fighting with the now-heavier weight of the sled. "I've told you to stop doing that!" He grips Hugo's harness in a firm clasp, all while struggling to keep the toboggan from slipping down the hill with me in it.

Hugo hops out of the toboggan, and my stomach flip-flops as the sled tilts to its right. Nico releases his hold on the dog's harness, snaring the horns of the toboggan while planting both skis firmly in the powder.

We're both breathing hard—him from exertion and me from alarm—when Nico finally steadies us. I look over to see Hugo sitting pretty, his tongue lolling to the side, as if the last two minutes never happened.

"That dog is going to be the death of me one day," Nico says, shaking his helmeted head. "You good?" He gestures to my ankle. Hugo's weight can't have been good for the injury.

I give my foot a wiggle. "It doesn't feel any worse than it did before. I'm good."

"Let's roll. This weather is shit. We've wasted too much time already."

Ouch. My silly infatuation is decidedly one-sided.

I know it's for the best, though. I have nothing to offer another person right now. I'm wrung out, and today is simply a fluke.

Nico shoves off his planted foot, taking a smooth glide forward. The toboggan hasn't moved an inch when we hear a hideous cracking noise, followed by two loud snaps. Hugo is on high alert, and his handler isn't any more relaxed. I lean to the left, peering around Nico's wide shoulders to get a better look.

Several yards in front of us, I see a large, fallen fir tree, laying clear across the trail in front of us. If we hadn't stopped to get Hugo off my lap, that tree might have been on top of us.

For the first time, I feel genuine fear. More than I had when I was on that hill all alone, thinking no one was coming.

"H—how are we going to get around that?"

Nico shakes his head. "We're not."

CHAPTER THREE

Wren

I LOOK UP AT Nico, as if staring at the blank canvas of his ski mask and goggles will give me some sort of clue about what he's thinking.

"What do you mean we're not getting around the tree? We *have* to get around the tree. How else will we get to the lodge?"

"We're not going to the lodge. Not anymore."

"Well, we're not staying out here."

A muffled growl-like sound comes from under Nico's layers. I've pissed him off—or the situation has.

"I know we're not staying out here, Wren. If you'd stop talking for a minute and just let me think, I'll tell you my plan."

I clench my teeth. "Fine. Do tell, wise ski man."

A mask can't roll its eyes, but somehow, his gives that impression.

"There's a small patrol cabin not far off. We mostly use it to store spare equipment and supplies. It's old, but it's got electricity and a wood stove. We're not taking a chance on this route. I don't trust the look of some of those other trees. Not in this weather."

The patrol cabin sounds cold and unappealing—and too cramped for two adults and one massive dog.

"If you're worried about the liability," I tell him, "I'll let you off the hook. I'd much rather be back at the lodge."

His frame tenses. "Do you think I don't know what I'm doing? I'm the one responsible for your safety. If I say we're not going around the tree, we're not going around the tree. You can risk your ass on your own time, but you won't do it on mine."

Well, then. "Fine."

He turns back toward the fallen tree, taking one last, lingering look at the obstacle before gliding forward and giving Hugo a command. The smiling dog trots beside me as we veer onto an offshoot of the trail.

We don't say a word to each other, the sound of the toboggan and Nico's skis cutting through the snowpack making an awkward soundtrack.

A brutal dose of wind tunnels through the narrow trail we're now on. As worried as I am about being trapped in a tiny supply cabin during a storm, I know Nico is right.

We have no choice but to take shelter in the nearest structure we can find.

I'll worry about being in close quarters with another person after we get there. I've lost track of how to interact with people—or at least ones not mandated by mutual grief to speak with me.

And anyway, I've already pissed this man off. It isn't like I have anything to lose if he sees who I really am—broken and sad and lonely.

We will make it through this storm together. I'll finish my task, and then we will never see each other again.

I clear my throat. "How far until we get to this cabin?"

"Less than three minutes."

The exact answer matches the precision with which he moves. There's a natural grace to him, even as he tows me behind him. I've only ever known one person who skied like that. But beyond their skiing, the two couldn't be more different.

I flick another look at my watch, deciding to test Nico and his exactitude. He won't even know I'm doing it.

I press the small button on the side of the watch face, setting a timer for two-and-a-half minutes.

Smiling to myself, I tuck my hands under my legs and settle in to enjoy the rest of the ride.

"You good back there?"

"Huh?" I blink my eyes rapidly, looking up to find Nico's head turned to look at me. He quickly looks back in front of us then toward me again.

"You were quiet."

"I fell asleep, I guess."

"Don't do that again."

"It's not like I planned it."

"Don't care. You need to be alert. We're almost to the cabin. You can relax as much as you want when we get there."

It's hard to resent him when he's right. I can't believe I dozed off. My timer hasn't gone off, so I know it hasn't even been two minutes.

I wiggle my limbs, stretching them as far as they can go in the compact sled. I stretch my head back, loosening the taut muscles in my neck and shoulders.

"We're here."

I sit up straight. We're in front of a small, utilitarian-looking cabin. A dark-green metal roof tops the faded-brown outer walls. A rectangular white sign that identifies the shack as Holly Peak Ski Patrol sits between a small window and a narrow door. Hugo gives a woof before bounding up the two steps that lead to the entry.

I shiver as another streak of cold air cuts through my jacket. "Is it warm inside?"

Nico looks back at me as he releases his boot bindings. He steps out of his skis and pulls a set of keys from one of his vest pockets. "The wood-burning stove will take a while to get things warmed up. We'll need to stay bundled up for a bit."

He pushes open the door, stows our skis inside, then glances back at me. I'm still in the toboggan.

"You coming or what?"

He's impatient, and I don't blame him. He must think I'm absolutely insane.

"Um, I'm not sure I can get out of this thing on my own."

He doesn't hesitate or grumble as he stalks over to the sled. I catch sight of Hugo sitting in the doorway just over Nico's left shoulder.

My watch timer sounds right as Nico crouches down.

He pauses. "What's that?"

I fumble with the buttons, my gloves making my fingers clumsy.

"N—nothing," I say as I finally hit the right combination to silence it.

My companion's head tilts to the side. "Were you timing me?"

"Uh...maybe?"

I've never wanted to see another person's face more than I want to see his in this moment. Is he smiling or scowling? Straight-faced or fighting a smirk? Does one of his lips curl up at the corner when he is reluctantly amused?

Or is he just annoyed and sick of me already?

"Well, are you impressed?" he asks darkly. His voice has lowered an octave, rumbling from the depths of his chest. It's a wonder I can even make out the words.

My mouth drops open, my stomach diving as he sweeps me off my feet and out of the toboggan.

This last year, I've lost weight. I'm thinner than I've ever been in my life. But I'm still tall. Carrying me shouldn't be easy, but somehow Nico makes it feel that way. I imagine there is a solid layer of sinew underneath all the bright red and reflective tape.

"You don't have to carry me," I say, hoping he misses the breathlessness in my tone.

"Yeah, I do." He pauses. "It's my job to take care of you."

No one has taken care of me for a long time. Not for nine years. I want to lie down in this feeling, wrap it around me and zip myself inside like a sleeping bag.

Nico is just doing his job, though, and I'm nothing special. But I'll remember him for the rest of my life.

He crosses the threshold of the cabin, and my head nearly hits the door frame.

"Sorry," he grunts.

"You can put me down." He carted me around in that toboggan, powering us through the trails against wind and blowing snow. He must be exhausted.

"Not until I get you a chair."

"How are you going to do that while you're holding me? I can stand, Nico, I promise."

My body moves with him as his chest heaves with a heavy sigh. "Alright. But you'd better stand completely still. Not a single step. Got it?"

"Got it," I mumble.

This is new. He's ordering me around but in a caring way. I've been on my own for the last year, and before that, I was the one doing all the caretaking, all the being firm and advocating and pushing, pushing, pushing.

Nico finally places me on my feet. I balance on one foot, careful to keep the weight off the injured one. Hugo nudges my dangling hand, offering me some stability.

"Thanks for your help today, big guy," I tell him quietly.

The dog looks up at me expectantly, commanding my attention the same way his handler does. "You sure are bossy, aren't you?"

I tug off my gloves, sinking my fingers into his thick fur.

"You'll want to keep the gloves on until I get the stove going."

I look toward Nico, who is now standing behind me, his hands wrapped around the back of a rolling desk chair. He hasn't removed a single layer.

"Sit," he says.

I lower into the seat. "Yes, sir."

He stills, but the blue-black of his goggles offers no clue as to his thoughts. I want him to think I'm funny, but I'm not a funny person.

I'm grumpy, and sad, and sometimes mean.

Marcqui would yell at me for describing myself that way.

Challenge those thoughts, she would say. *You are not your feelings, Wren.*

But that's easier said than done, and Marcqui isn't here right now. It's only me, and my knight, and his noble steed.

As Nico works at the wood-burning stove, I look around the cabin for the first time. It's cluttered and unattractive, but someone clearly tidies it on a semi-regular basis.

The walls are stark, with only an empty bulletin board and a faded trail map adorning the wood grain. Someone has also tacked up a tiny, white piece of paper with a hand-drawn map of Holly Hill. The main part of the cabin is an open room, but there is a small office toward the right where I can make out a messy desk and an exam bed.

A rectangular folding table is shoved against the wall opposite the stove. On top, I see an electric kettle. The power cord dangles freely off to the side. A large orange jug—like one an athlete would dump all over their coach after a championship win—sits next to it.

There are two doors along the back wall, one that Nico identifies as a very rudimentary bathroom, *hot water not included*. The other door is labeled with a small sign that says: *Supply Closet*.

Hugo rests his head on my knee as I absentmindedly gaze out the window. The snow is coming down even harder than it was when Nico carried me inside. We're not getting out of here anytime soon. A wooden A-frame cabin is visible in the distance with a stack of pale-gray smoke rising from its chimney. It looks cozy—certainly cozier than the cluttered cabin that Nico and I are in.

"Who lives there?" I ask.

He turns his head at the question. If goggles could look irritated, his do. I've interrupted his concentration at the wood stove, apparently. I don't know what he's doing, but he seems to have a strict system for whatever it is. His movements are brisk and efficient, his uncovered hands a smooth blur of motion. If he would only hold still for longer than a second, I could study those hands and that sparest hint of naked skin.

I'm thirsty and pathetic, lusting over the one small scrap of this man that I can see.

"That's Willow's place," he eventually replies.

Is this how people feel when I talk to them? The brief answers that don't offer any actual information? Then again, I asked a closed-ended question. I've observed enough of Marcqui's tricks in counseling to know that those aren't the kind that invite real responses.

Not unless the person actually wants to talk, which the grouchy ski patroller clearly does not.

"Looks warm over there."

"Yep."

He grabs a few pieces of wood from the stack by the door, shoves them in, and firmly shuts the stove. The immediate burst of warmth has me unwrapping the scarf from around my neck and pulling the goggles up and over my helmet. I undo my chin strap and tug both the helmet and my beanie off at the same time.

I'm shaking out my hair when I feel it.

Nico's attention is squarely on me. His whole body is tense beneath his thick red jacket.

My fingers running over my scalp still. "Are you okay?" I ask.

I watch a full-body shiver run over him before he clears his throat. "Thought I told you to keep everything on until I was finished." His voice sounds huskier than it did before. I have no idea how to read him right now.

"Aren't you? Finished, I mean?" I gesture toward the stove, which continues to pump heat into the cabin.

He nods once before stepping into the office area. I try not to listen as I hear him saying something over his handheld radio, his smooth murmur followed by a garbled reply. My stomach dips when Nico chuckles under his breath, deep and low.

"So," I whisper to the dog crouched at my feet, "how long do you think we'll be in here for?"

Hugo looks up at me with those big brown eyes as I rub under his chin. I smile at the bit of drool growing at the corner of his mouth. I count it as a win that I've won over Nico's dog, despite the human's obvious reluctance to be anywhere near me.

"At least another few hours."

I startle. Nico stands in the opening connecting the office to the larger, open area of the cabin. He props his right shoulder on the inner edge of the door frame, one booted ankle crossed over the other. He's as casual as I've seen him yet, but it feels deceptive, like he's only lying in wait. For what, I don't know.

I swallow as he uncurls from that leaning pose, walking the few steps toward me. He stops a pace or two in front of where my feet rest on the floor.

"Come on," he says, tipping his head behind him to the office. "I need to look at that ankle."

H E CLEARS A PILE of junk—boxes of bandages and earplugs and tongue depressors—from off the exam table. I decline his offer to boost me up onto the cold vinyl. Scooting my way into the room in the rolling chair was already undignified enough.

I wonder if the remaining chill in the air is the reason Nico still hasn't uncovered himself at all. The impenetrable shell of ski mask and goggles covers his face. He's removed the helmet at least, though a thick black beanie covers all hints of hair beneath.

Maybe he is ugly, like some scarred Gothic anti-hero of old. One that doesn't let the heroine see his face until the emotional climax of the story, only for her to faint at the sight of his no-more-than-mildly unsettling pockmarks.

I wouldn't care, and I certainly wouldn't faint. Nico could be hideous, with lopsided eyes and a bent nose, and it wouldn't matter one bit. Because something about him makes me feel alive for the first time in years. It may only be one-sided, and he may simply be doing his job, but it still feels special. So special I can only recall one time I have ever felt this way. That didn't work out, but it's good to know the feeling isn't a one-and-done thing.

Maybe when I finish this thing for Dad, I'll get back on the dating scene. The thought is enough to have me snickering.

"Gonna unlace the boot now, alright?"

The words pull me from my thoughts, and I nod at my faceless rescuer. His bare fingers move nimbly over the laces, not shaking in the slightest. It isn't the chill keeping him locked away.

He seems to brace himself before pushing up the bottom of my colorful pant leg and pulling my boot and sock down in two swift motions, touching me as little as possible.

It's clinical. Detached.

This is Nico's job, and if he had used a medical exam as an opportunity to get touchy, I wouldn't like him at all, his sexy voice and its strange effect on me be damned.

"Ready?" he asks.

I look down to where he is kneeling at my feet. He is poised to grasp the ankle that I now see is slightly swollen. Oddly enough, I can hardly feel the injury any longer, though only a short time ago, it left me unable to stand.

A sick part of my brain wants to ask him, "*Do you feel this too?*" Instead, I settle for a nod and assure him I am ready.

A full-body shiver travels from the tip of my toes to the crown of my head when his fingers curl around the naked arch of my foot.

He pulls away just as quickly as he removed my boot.

"Did that hurt?"

I shake my head. It didn't. Not at all. But how can I possibly explain my completely inappropriate attraction to this man without making him wildly uncomfortable?

"I'm just nervous," I say. It's the most plausible explanation I can come up with on the spot.

He accepts it, grasping my foot again in a warm hold, manipulating it gently in different directions as he asks me a series of formal questions about how each motion makes me feel.

Good. Fine. Hurts a little. A five on a scale of one to ten. Dull. Achy.

If he could dive deep into my soul, my answers would be of an entirely different character. Answers not about my ankle and pain but about the smooth touch of his lightly callused fingertips along my skin. About the strength evident in his gentle grip. About the thick veins in his hands and his long, dexterous fingers.

Off-kilter. Fluttery. Breathless. Swept off my feet. The list could go on.

"All done." He gives my ankle a cursory pat atop the layer of wound fabric bandage he placed on it.

"Oh." I hadn't even noticed him finishing the exam, too far off in my musings. "Thank you."

"Want to try bearing weight on it?"

I hesitate. What if I fall flat on my face? Again. Only this time, in front of this man and his adorable dog.

"If it's too much too soon, I'll carry you," he offers, sensing my reluctance.

That's what I'm afraid of. There is no way I can manage being that close to Nico again without giving away the thoughts running through my head.

"I, uh...I guess I'm just a little nervous still."

He tilts his head thoughtfully, not unlike the way Hugo looked at me earlier. He's still crouched below me, one wrist resting casually across a knee. "Are you nervous about your ankle, or is it because of me?"

Oh, fuck. Is my weird crush on him that obvious? I thought I'd been doing a good job of hiding it.

"I—I...it's only that you're wearing a mask," I end up saying. It's half-truth, half-lie, but believable enough. "Who wouldn't be a little nervous around a guy wearing a mask?"

He doesn't utter a word, but I stare, breathless, as he takes both hands to the straps of his goggles and lifts them up and off. Before I can process it, he's sliding the black ski mask over his head. He rises to his feet, his thick, dark hair settling in waves around his ears.

My eyes follow the planes of his face, his jet-black hair, those dark eyes that tilt up slightly in the corners, the sharp slope of his nose, and the layer of stubble along his firm jaw.

I fall back on the exam table, my shoulder blades smacking the wall behind me. Suddenly, it's not just my ankle that's throbbing but my chest as well.

Because the face I'm looking at is not only devastatingly beautiful but horrifyingly familiar.

"Dom?"

CHAPTER FOUR

Nico

I HAVEN'T SEEN WREN Dunbar in almost nine years. I knew it was Wren on that hill the second I came peeling around the corner and heard her laughing with Hugo's nose buried in her neck.

That used to be my favorite spot on her to smell. Something about the way her shampoo and perfume mingled in the curve of her shoulder.

Here I am, jealous of my own fucking dog.

If I hadn't recognized Wren's laugh, I would have known her by those ski pants that she still hasn't gotten rid of. The obnoxious clash of colors was the reason I'd first talked to her all those years ago.

I'd seen her and her friends on the mountain on the first day of my trip, mesmerized by the way two gingery-blonde strands of hair dangled from her beanie and framed her slightly freckled face.

I may as well have been invisible to her until I cracked a joke about those ugly pants and made her laugh.

Her group of friends and mine mingled together after that. That night, I asked her to meet me in the lobby of the ski lodge where we talked the entire night through, sipping cheap, instant hot cocoa by the fire. I kissed her on the second day, not wanting to waste another minute. We were inseparable for the rest of the trip.

Even our attendance at colleges two hours apart hadn't stopped our connection. For a full year, we would call each other on the phone before bed, catching up about our days. On weekends, we would alternate on who visited whom.

Being Wren's boyfriend had been the high point of my life...until she vanished, leaving me with a note and a disconnected phone number. I've alternated between angry with her and worried for her so often over the years that I've never been sure where to settle.

But seeing her on that hill, flat on her back with my dog beside her, I realized I never settled without her, not one bit.

I'm still mad, and worried, and for the first time in years, hopeful about something.

From the look on Wren's face, hopeful isn't anywhere in her equation.

I can't say I wasn't at least a little hurt that she didn't recognize me the way I did her, but she knows me now, and she's not happy about it.

And maybe, just maybe, I kept my identity hidden as long as I did to punish her for the hurt I felt so long ago.

"Hey, Wren," I say. It's woefully inadequate.

I don't expect her to laugh, but she does. There is no humor in it, though, only bitterness and perhaps a hint of sadness. Disappointment.

Well, I guess now she finally knows how it feels.

It doesn't satisfy me the way I once imagined.

When the laughter is all pushed out of Wren's lungs, she hits me with a watery glare from those green eyes.

"You're a sick fuck, you know that?"

I take a step back at the quiet force of her anger. Hugo lopes into the room, roused by the stirring emotion. He whines when he notices Wren struggling to get down from the exam table.

"Careful." I reach out a hand.

She cuts me off wordlessly, her mouth set in a tight line.

"You don't get to tell me to be careful, Dom. Or Nico. Or whatever the hell your name is."

"You can call me whatever you'd like, Wren."

Her dangling feet touch the floor. She's still holding most of her weight with her hands on the table. I watch like a hawk as she tests the limits of her injured ankle.

"How about I call you Liar, then? I like the sound of that one."

I shake my head slowly. I deserve that, but I also deserve a chance to explain.

"My name isn't a lie. No one calls me Dom anymore."

The truth is, I'm not the same guy Wren used to know. Dom was my past self. He was restless and reckless, a walking disaster.

Nico is steady and cautious. He follows the rules and takes care of the people he loves, even if they don't like it.

"Cool story, *Nico*."

I'd forgotten the biting power of a pissed-off Wren.

She grabs the back of the rolling desk chair, using it as a makeshift walker, and slowly limps her way past me.

She holds her head high and straight, ignoring me entirely.

Her shoulder brushes mine, and she shies away.

I turn and follow the path of her movements with my eyes.

She's thin in a way that makes me worried. She'd always been trim and athletic, but now she looks almost gaunt. Those hideous ski pants are looser on her than they ever used to be.

I wonder who, if anyone, is taking care of Wren these days. I wonder if Wren is even taking care of Wren.

Her presence alone on a mountain trail in the middle of a massive snowstorm tells me enough to make an educated guess.

Hugo casts me a sidelong look before trailing Wren out of the exam room.

Even my dog is disappointed in me.

I grab the other desk chair, the one with the rusty wheel and the crooked armrest, and roll it in to sit next to Wren.

This time, I'm prepared for the icy glare she shoots my way.

"It's too cold in the office," I explain.

Her only response is to fold her arms over her chest and twist her chair slightly to the left.

Dom would have scooted closer, nudged her with his boot.

But I'm older now, more analytical. I've had to be in my line of work. If I push her too fast, Wren will retreat further. And even though I'm still mad as hell at her for disappearing on me all those years ago, I'd rather be mad at the Wren in front of my face than risk never seeing her again.

"How's the ankle?" I ask, out of altruism but also to fill the tense silence.

"So-so," she says in a flat voice.

"What does that mean?"

She peers at me sideways. I want to smile but decide not to risk my neck.

"It means it's not good, but not bad. So-so."

"Want a Tylenol? I'd offer Ibuprofen, but..." She's allergic.

Her head whips toward me in question.

"I do know you, Wren."

That bitter laugh tears up from her throat again, and I hate it so much. I stand, wanting to pace, but there's no room.

We're stuck together, and she hates me.

"Want some coffee?" I ask. "I want some coffee."

I sift through the supply closet, pushing past a layer of blankets to find one of the large, five-gallon water jugs stored in the front. This cabin isn't used often, but I make sure it's stocked with all the essentials just in case. The younger patrollers, all green volunteers, like to tease me about it, but in moments like this, it pays off.

I'll gloat once the storm is over. Then, I'll turn it into a training exercise. I'll need to get on them for stacking too many things on top of one another. Getting anything out of the back of the closet is going to be a nightmare.

Momentarily distracted at the thought, I almost forget Wren is behind me. I turn, straining as I carry the heavy jug toward the table with the electric kettle. She looks away but not before I catch her staring.

"Interested in a cup?" I ask as I fill the kettle.

I turn it on, breathing a tiny sigh of relief that the storm hasn't kicked off the power. This cabin is close enough to the main resort building that we're on the same grid.

"Instant?"

"Yep."

She wrinkles her nose, and I laugh. "Sorry, it's not exactly Snowcap quality. But it's all I've got."

The kettle beeps to show the water has reached the ideal temperature.

"I went there, you know." Her statement surprises me.

I glance behind me. Wren is careful not to watch as I fill our paper cups, stirring in the instant coffee mixture.

"Where? Snowcap, you mean?"

The turn of conversation is disjointed, but maybe Wren dislikes our silence as much as I do. We never used to be quiet when we were together. We would talk and laugh and talk some more.

"Yeah." She thanks me with a nod when I pass her the steaming cup. Her fingertips are cool against mine, and suddenly I'm envious of the fact that the coffee will be what warms them instead of my hands.

I clear my throat. "It's good, isn't it? Snowcap? The owner there—Alice—does a lot for the community."

"She was...nice." She says it like nice is a dirty word.

"Yeah. She's cool."

Wren sips her coffee, the steam wrapping around the harsh lines of her cheekbones.

"Are you dating her?" she asks.

I nearly inhale my coffee. "Who? Alice? No. I'm...not dating anyone."

I tried after Wren left, but nothing ever lasted. Then, after a while, I stopped trying.

Wren nods, as if my single status holds some vast, profound knowledge.

"What about you? Are you...dating someone?" Someone who might give a shit that she's stranded in a cabin with her ex-boyfriend for God knows how long?

She snickers as if my question isn't just as absurd and out of place as her own. "I am very much not dating anyone."

"Oh. Okay."

Selfishly, I'm glad she's unattached. But the sadness, the sheer loneliness behind her words, hits me hard.

This Wren is a shadow of my Wren.

We sip in silence for a bit, the only sounds those of the wood stove crackling and Hugo snoring.

"Why did you do it, Dom?"

My grip on the coffee cup tightens, and my chest feels like it's caving in. She doesn't need to specify what she means.

"I had to get you off the trail."

I hear her sharp intake of breath. Her rage is building up again. I look over to see her, red-cheeked and alive. I'll take that anger as long as she looks alive.

"And you didn't think you could do that without completely lying to me? And don't give me some shit about how everyone calls you by your new name, as if that makes you any less of a liar."

"It was...an omission, not a lie. And can you honestly tell me you would have come with me if I'd told you who I was right away? There was no good decision for me to make there, Wren. It was either fight you then, or fight you now. At least I know you're warm and safe this way."

"I would have come with you, Dom. I'm not an idiot, and I don't have a death wish."

"Don't you?"

Her face pales, the freckles stark against her skin. The rage is stifled, replaced by naked fear.

"What were you doing alone on top of a mountain in the middle of a snowstorm, Wren?" I tread softly, my words scarcely louder than a whisper.

Her mouth drops open. I think she's going to tell me, to open up, but she only twists away in her chair.

"It's none of your damn business, Nico." She drags out the last syllable of my name, like she's sampling how it feels on her tongue.

"How is that not my business? I'm the one who risked my ass to get you safe." I don't tell her I would have done it for anyone. I definitely don't tell her that I especially would have done it for her.

"I don't know you. I'm not about to divulge my deepest, darkest secrets to a stranger."

"So, it's something deep and dark, then, huh?" She rolls those green eyes, some of that fighting spirit shining through once more.

"Hardly."

"Since you insist on insulting us both by calling me a stranger, why don't I tell you something deep and dark about me in return."

I have no idea where the idea came from, but once I voice it, I like it more and more.

That's when she hits me where it hurts. If there is one thing I remember about Wren, it's her ability to cut.

"I doubt there's anything deep about you."

That might have been true once. I was the clown, the jester, the goofy guy who lived to make his friends laugh. But it was all a front for the secret worry that no one in my life took me seriously.

Wren took me seriously once. I wonder if she left because she realized her mistake.

I sip my gritty coffee, running my tongue over my teeth before wading into the sparring ring. "See you still haven't outgrown that bitchy streak of yours."

She crosses her arms over her chest. I never used to call her out so directly, and she's not prepared for it.

But I like the way the fire in her eyes has run off some of the sadness.

"I'm not a nice person anymore."

I shrug. "Me neither."

She scoffs. "Please. You make a living rescuing people, and you have an adorable furball of a dog. You're *nice*."

"Was I nice when I lied to you?" *When I used that opportunity to get my petty revenge?*

"Ah! So, you do admit that you lied after all! That it wasn't simply an *omission* about your name."

"I'd lie again if it got us here."

She wrinkles her brow. I'm getting too close too fast. It's like the night we first met at the ski lodge, when we couldn't stop talking to each other even if we'd wanted to. Back then, she liked it.

Now she's spitting mad, but she still can't help herself.

She uncrosses her arms and spins her chair around in a slow circle, lofting her empty coffee cup into the garbage can in the corner.

It makes a perfect arc, landing with a muffled clang in the metal bin. Wren is still annoyingly athletic. I'm sure if I had found her before she was flat on her back in the snow, she would have skied circles around me. She was always the epitome of a ripper, crazy good without even trying.

"Go ahead, then. Tell me about how dark *Nico's* life has been."

I rub my hand over my jaw to hide my smile. My gambit worked.

"You sure you're ready? Don't forget, you agreed to return the favor with your own deep and dark. I want to know why you're in Holly Hill and why you were out alone in the middle of the worst storm I've seen in five years."

She rolls her eyes, but her chest is rising and falling rapidly, her lips quirking. I think she might be having fun.

"Do I have any other choice? It's not as if I'm going anywhere," she says with a gesture around the cabin.

I shrug. She makes a valid point. "Fine. I moved to Holly Hill because I have PTSD and couldn't do my job anymore."

Her lips purse and relax. I watch her mouth form the letter S, but I don't let her get that far.

"Don't apologize. Don't treat me differently now."

It's my biggest pet peeve when people act like I am either a delicate flower who can't handle an ounce of stress or a dangerous pressure cooker that's about to burst.

"What was your job? Before this, I mean."

She's clearly struggling to reconcile the guy I used to be, the one who wanted nothing more than to remain free of obligations, with the sort of guy who had to be *forced* out of a job.

I shake my head. "Nah. It's your turn."

She sighs. "I guess I'm supposed to tell you why I'm in Holly Hill too."

My nonchalance is feigned when I beckon for her to go ahead. I'm desperate to know how she got here. How she ended up in my little town, on my ski trail, with my dog.

"I'm here because my dad died."

Fuck.

I met Wren's dad only once during the year we dated. The distance between her college and mine and her hometown made regular visits difficult.

What I remember is he was a nice guy who enjoyed fishing, and hiking, and most of all, skiing. Wren was raised by a single dad. The two of them talked on the phone every night.

"I'm—"

"Nope. Don't even say it. You didn't want my apology, so I don't want yours either."

I ask the only question I can think to ask next. "How are you? Really?"

"It's your turn."

I crane my neck, loosening some of the tension I'm holding there. The room is growing hot, the wood-burning stove continuing to pump out heat. I unzip my red ski patrol jacket, unfastening my various straps and pouches before leaning forward to pull it down my arms. The black, lightweight fleece jacket I'm left wearing is similar to the one Wren has on, though hers is a muted pink.

"You wanted to know my job before I moved here, right?"

She raises her brows, like she knows I'm stalling.

To her credit, I am. I hate talking about my old job. Not because I miss it so much, but because *I* used to *be* my job, and now I don't even recognize the person I was when I did it.

"I was a wildland firefighter."

She sits at attention, turning fully toward me. "What happened to starting your own outdoor adventure company?"

Wren knew more about my old plans than anyone else. I'd been muddling my way through school, struggling with general education classes and intro to business coursework. Like a proper ski bum, all I really cared about was skiing and finding a way to do that as much as possible.

"Didn't pan out. I realized pretty quick it was just an excuse to be outside and fuck around. There are people killing it in that industry now, but it wasn't for me."

"So, the firefighting? Doesn't sound like much fucking around."

She's cheating at our little game, but I decide to ignore it. "You'd be surprised at some of the things we got up to on our downtime. The pay was shit, and summers were hell. But I traveled a lot and got decent government benefits. It evened out most of the time."

Right until I couldn't even myself out anymore. I have more good days than bad days now, at least. But I had to leave that environment entirely to make it this far.

"How long were you—"

I've overlooked it for long enough. I want her to know these things about me, but I'm a greedy bastard when it comes to Wren, and I want more of *her*.

"When did your dad pass away?"

She grimaces. "I hate that phrase. *He passed away.* Can't people stop with the euphemisms and call it what it is? Dead. My dad is dead."

"Okay." It sounds harsh to my ears, but I'm not the one living her grief. Wren's sadness is palpable. If she wants to say her dad *died*, I'll say it that way. If she wants me to say he shuffled off his mortal coil and became a constellation in the sky, I'll say that too. "When did your dad die?"

"A year ago, today."

For the second time in a row, all I can think is *Fuck*.

Her being up here is a way to be close to her dad, doing the activity they both loved. It makes sense that she'd feel like she had to ski the trails today, despite the storm raging around us.

I know *why* she was on the trail now. But I still don't fully grasp the connection between her dad and Holly Hill. I picked this town because it was quiet. Good skiing, low risk of wildfires. The worst sort of natural disaster we get in Holly Hill is an ice or snow storm—much like the one that struck today.

I found Holly Hill by chance. Hugo and I had taken a camping trip, hiking along trails in the Northeast. I'd heard there was a good craft beer scene in town, found the ski resort, and fell in love with the pace of life here.

It might be slow, but I like slow these days. I *need* slow these days.

"Had your dad ever been to Holly Hill before?"

She nods. "That's why I picked it. It might sound lame, but he had this picture of him and all his friends here from back in the day. Their high school did a trip every year. This was where he fell in love with skiing. He talked about bringing me here one day, but, well...that didn't happen."

"Was he sick?"

She shoots out of her chair, causing it to roll back a few feet. Hugo lifts his head from the makeshift pillow he's made himself out of a pile of old blankets.

She wobbles, and I'm on my feet with a hand at her elbow to steady her.

"Careful. You don't want to aggravate that ankle."

She's breathing rapidly, staring up at me with pinprick pupils. Her pulse thrums in her throat.

This is different from how she looked during our back-and-forth volley. I'm intimately familiar with the way she looks now, because I've seen it in the mirror more times than I can count.

Wren is terrified, and her fear response has kicked into overdrive.

I should ask if it's okay with her, but I don't. I just pull her in close, bringing her cheek to the center of my chest. It's second nature when I feel the way her soft strands of hair tangle in my fingers. How the cool, minty scent of her shampoo mixes with the tang of fresh snow. It's just like before, only tinged with time and grief.

I breathe in low through my mouth, letting my diaphragm fill with air, sitting in the near-discomfort of overfull lungs. I'll never tire of breathing fresh, smoke-free air. Once it starts to really hurt, I blow out through my nose, letting it all go.

Wren catches on quicker than I hoped. By the third cycle of breaths, she's doing it with me. Two more, and the muscles in the arm I'm still gripping have slackened. I slide that hand over her upper arm, up and up until my hand is in the center of her back. Others might like slow circles, to be rubbed and caressed. Wren was always fonder of firm pressure, so that's what I give her.

I may not have been good at anything else when Wren and I dated before, but I knew exactly how to love her. And it seems I never forgot.

CHAPTER FIVE

Wren

DOMINIC DI LAURO—DOM, NICO, whatever name he's call-ing himself—smells amazing. Like a warm, cozy mug of hot chocolate by the fireplace. It's not cologne or laundry detergent or anything I can name. Smelling him makes me feel the way I felt when Dad and I would put on fuzzy socks, warm from the dryer, curl up on opposite ends of the couch, and watch the Winter Olympics.

The Games had aired last year, not even two months after he died, and all I could do was sob into the arm of that same empty couch.

In the middle of the slalom event, I'd looked up names of local realtors. The house sold before the closing ceremony.

With money from the sale and the modest lump sum Dad left me, I bought my hatchback, grabbed Dad's old notebook with the list of every place he'd skied, and booked a room at the first resort on the list. Over the last ten months, I've gotten more organized on my travels. At first, I'd been all over the place: a stay in Vermont one week, then back out West two weeks later. After that, I'd gotten out a map, plotting my way on strategic points, making sure I'd hit up each resort during the best time of year.

I was efficient about it until Holly Peak. This was always going to be the last stop, the place where Dad's love of skiing started.

And somehow, out of every resort under the sun, this is the one where my ex-boyfriend works.

I don't know how or why I ended up in Nico's arms, but he feels like...home.

A shock wave of heat flashes in my gut, and I pull my head away.

How can I feel this way about Nico when he lied to me? When we have the history that we do and it would never, ever work?

When he lives here in Holly Hill, settled and saving lives, while I'm about to be rudderless as soon as the contents of the sandwich bag in my jacket pocket are emptied.

"Thanks," I tell him.

He helped me, doing the breathwork thing. Marcqui has shown us that technique before in group, and we've practiced it at the end of sessions. But I've never felt it in person. It was...nice to feel connected that way.

I step back gingerly, testing the limits of my ankle. The wrap Nico put on it helps, and the painkillers are doing enough to take the edge off.

It's hard to read the look in his eyes. He's so different from the guy I used to know, but he looks nearly the same. His facial hair is thicker, his black hair a touch longer. There are new lines around his eyes—a remnant from squinting into bright snow—and at the corners of his mouth. The lines turn down, and I wonder how often he's had cause to smile in the last few years.

He likely hasn't, considering his old line of work. Dom used to run from stress, barely making it to class most days unless I called him to get him out of bed. He would answer the phone, laughing every time, never embarrassed, just happy to hear my voice first thing in the morning. I would act annoyed, but I secretly loved hearing him laugh like that. Our best conversations happened on those mornings, when he'd put me on speakerphone while he rushed to throw on sweats and brush his teeth. We would talk about the future, about all the fun we would have, Dom starting up some amorphous company that was really just an excuse to be on the slopes, and me working seasonal jobs at the resorts.

Even if I hadn't left, those kids never would have lasted. We had no plan, no life experience. All we had was insane chemistry and an inexplicable connection.

He finally shrugs off my thanks, the angles of his cheeks tinted pink. "Don't mention it. You want another cup of coffee?"

I really, really don't want to choke down another cup of instant coffee. Nico had overloaded his with sugar to disguise the taste just like he always used to, but I take my mine black. There's no hiding the taste with plain, black coffee.

The meal I had this morning at Snowcap Café is a distant fantasy at this point.

My stomach growls as if on cue. "Is there any food in this place?"

"Yeah. Sit tight."

I settle back in my rolling chair, listening to Nico rummage around in a large standing cabinet. Hugo opens one of his big brown eyes, giving me a look that can only be described as beseeching. I giggle under my breath, using my non-injured foot to scoot my chair closer to where the large dog is lying.

He rolls shamelessly onto his belly, his tongue flopping out of his mouth as he wiggles. I was on the verge of crying a few minutes ago, and now I can't wipe the smile off my face.

Maybe I need to get a dog.

"He's not going to let you stop doing that," Nico tosses over his shoulder.

"That's fine. I like him."

"He's actually a therapy dog."

"He is?"

Nico strides over, carrying two paper plates full of various snacks. I spot almonds, some dried cranberries and apricots, a scoop of trail mix, and a small stack of crackers. It's the rustic version of a charcuterie board. I accept the plate he offers me, placing it on top of my knee. Nico lowers into the other chair, tossing a handful of almonds into his mouth.

"I thought he was a search-and-rescue dog?"

Nico nods before taking another swig from his mug. "He's that too. After I left the forest service, that's when I got the job out at that big resort in Wyoming. One of the avalanche dogs there had puppies, and this guy was one of them. He's got all his certifications, but as you saw on the trail, he's still learning."

I take my time chewing a dried apricot. "How many places have you lived?" We'd been in Colorado back when we were together.

"Too many. I started out in Colorado. Then Arizona, Wyoming, California. A little time in North Dakota. It was a lot of moving."

That sounds like the Dom I used to know. "So, you did get to have your adventures after all, then."

There's a sneer in my voice that I don't like—not after he divulged that his old career traumatized him. But I can't help but resent the fact that while I was stuck in the same monotonous loop every day for nearly nine years, Nico was running headlong into danger and adventure.

His eyes narrow to tiny slits. "What's that supposed to mean?"

A gust of wind rattles the walls of the cabin, sending a chill over my skin.

I tuck my hands under my thighs. "Nothing."

"It didn't sound like nothing. It sounded like a whole lot of something."

"You're reading into things."

"No, I don't think I am. Say what you mean, Wren."

"I told you it was nothing."

"I don't believe you."

"Why can't you just accept what I'm telling you?"

"Because I know you're lying. It's written all over your face."

I turn away, my jaw tightening as I watched the thick curtain of white snow whipping past the window. "Don't make assumptions. Maybe this is what my face looks like all the time."

I can hear his smirk. "Let's not act like we're strangers, Wren. I know what you look like when you're hiding something."

"How is that even possible? This is the first time you've seen me in years."

The air prickles. Outside, there's another snap and thud. More trees are coming down.

Suddenly, the wind quiets. There is only the noise of the wood crackling in the stove and Hugo's snuffling inhalations.

"Whose fault is that, Wren?"

Nico's voice is so heavy that I have to turn and look at him. I can't stop myself. Just like I can't stop myself from wanting to know everything about anything he's done the last nine years, even though he is right.

We are the way we are because of me.

I'm the one who put those shadows under his eyes. I'm the one responsible for the down-turned lines around his mouth and the bitterness in his tone. My fingers twitch. I lift my hand to reach for his...

A squawk comes from the office, and I startle. It's Nico's radio.

He's immediately in action, tossing his paper plate and moving toward the radio. Hugo isn't far behind, abandoning me to lope toward his owner.

"Yeah?" he says to the person on the other side.

"I've got bad news for you and that skier, Nico." It sounds like the same person who answered my call to dispatch earlier.

I can feel the weight of Nico's sigh from across the cabin. "Tell me, Shan." All I can see of him is his broad back. Hugo is steady at his side.

"The radar looks bad. Real bad. You're gonna have to stay put at least until tomorrow morning. We've got reports of people stuck in ditches all over the county. Why so many damn idiots think they can just disregard a travel ban is beyond me. It's like they think four-wheel drive makes them invincible or something."

"Okay, Shan. You remember this is an open channel, right? All the staff on the resort can hear you."

Shan swears under her breath, and I watch Nico's back shake the tiniest bit.

"Guess it's a good thing we've got a skeleton crew on today. You two good on supplies in the cabin?"

"Stocked it last week with the essentials."

There's a snicker over the radio. "You would. Well, let me know if you need anything. Not that I could do anything about it, but it's the thought that counts."

"Goodbye, Shan."

Nico's head tips back as the radio goes quiet. Hugo nudges his owner's hand with his nose, and Nico responds by running those long, strong fingers over the dog's head, tracing those floppy, furred ears in a delicate pattern.

My eyes blur as I follow the smooth, gliding motions.

The room sways, and the next thing I know, Nico is at my side, and Hugo at the other. Nico's brown eyes are wide and alert. He's that calm and collected ski patroller again, not my caring, angry, teasing, sometimes bitter, sometimes sweet Nico.

I shake my head to clear it. He isn't *my* anything. Not now and certainly never again. That conversation before the radio interrupted us proved it. There are too many feelings between Nico and me, ones that we could never sift through well enough to erase the past.

"When was the last time you slept?"

It's hard to remember. I pulled into a grocery store parking lot about halfway through the drive from Vermont to Holly Hill and napped for an hour. But consistent, continuous sleep?

It's been at least a few days.

"Yeah, that's answer enough. I'm getting the cot out of the storage closet. Just...stay upright until then."

He makes a hand gesture at Hugo, who stays plastered at the side of my chair. I have a babysitter who's a dog. I suppose it's preferable to the human kind.

Nico rummages around in the same closet where he got the water jug, the clanging and clattering doing more to keep me conscious than Hugo's licks and nudges.

A piercing metallic scrape followed by a muffled grunt has me turning.

Nico stands with his hands on his hips, staring at a large, folded cot frame like it's his mortal enemy.

"Sorry that took so long. No matter how many times I tell them to follow the storage guidelines, they never listen. This was shoved way in back with a bunch of shit in the way."

"Who is they?"

There I go again, being overly curious about anything and everything in this man's life.

The cot frame gives another shriek as he unfolds it and positions it near the wall. I hate sleeping in wide open spaces, and it sends a strange thrill through me that he remembers that.

"The volunteers. I should have double-checked, but god forbid I take a day off during the season to go to a single doctor's appointment."

Many of the larger resorts have paid patrol staff. But small ones, like Holly Peak, tend to rely on volunteers to make up their ski patrol. I've seen a wide gamut of organizational structures on my travels this past year.

"How many volunteers do you have?"

"Enough to get us by but less than I would like. Me and Shan, the woman on the radio, are the only paid team members on the resort, aside from the hospitality staff."

He laughs at the look of shock that must be evident on my face. "Yeah, I know, it's a lot. On top of that, Shan doesn't do any of the skiing anymore since she injured her back a couple years ago. So, it leaves me and a bunch of volunteers. Most are pretty good, though."

"Sounds like you could use some more help."

"Eh. Probably. The resort owners have been trying to hire someone for the last two seasons, but it's hard to attract people to the area. We're small. Not as exciting as some of the other places."

It doesn't sound like Nico is taking advantage of the relaxed change of pace that he needed when he moved to Holly Hill.

"Don't give me that look." He peers at me over the edge of a flat sleeping pad.

"What look?"

Hugo snorts, making clear his thoughts on my feigned innocence.

"The same one I get from my therapist about slowing down, recognizing my limits. That's what the off-season is for."

"I wouldn't know."

He shrugs before laying a black nylon sleeping bag down on top of the pad. Another blanket goes on top of that, followed by a small cushion at the head of the bed.

"Get some rest," he says, patting the makeshift bed with a flat palm.

"What will you do?" *Where will you sleep?* There is only one cot, only one sleeping bag, only one bed, and I'm not sure if being that close to Nico is a good idea.

"Write up an incident report. Let me know if you need me."

CHAPTER SIX

Nico

WREN LOOKS STRESSED, EVEN in her sleep. It's a state I'm all too familiar with. I want to fix it for her, to take away all the things causing her pain. Maybe it's my savior complex, or leftover feelings from years ago, but she felt so damn good in my arms that my head can't help but feel muddled.

She's right that I don't know her anymore, though. I've told her plenty about me today, but I can't help but notice how carefully she's avoiding giving any details about her own life. She knows about my job, and my travels, and even my dog.

The only thing I know about her is that she's beautiful, grief-stricken, and in the middle of doing something reckless.

I'm no closer to finding out why she left me, and Colorado, and the life we were planning together all those years ago.

Feeling like a creep watching her sleep, I wander over to the window near the cabin door. I'm greeted with a wall of white. Shan was right when she said the radar looked bad. It's been two hours since Wren fell asleep, and there's no end in sight. Wren and I won't be going anywhere until tomorrow at the earliest.

A rustling sound comes from behind me, and I turn to see Wren stirring. She reaches her arms above her head, her long torso stretching in an upward curve under the sleeping bag. I smile at the strands of ginger-blonde hair that rise from the static.

"Sleep good?" I ask.

She sits up slowly, twisting at the waist. It's a graceful movement, one that makes me want to slide my fingers up inside her pink shirt to feel the warmth of her skin under my hands.

She blinks slowly, hitting me with the full force of her dopey grin.

It's...unexpected. And bittersweet. I remember a lot about Wren, but I forgot how happy she is when she first wakes up. Like all her fierce edges are dulled before she remembers to sharpen them so she can face the rest of the day.

I've missed that, and I still don't know why Wren took that—took herself—away from me.

"Surprisingly, yes. This cot setup is more comfortable than it looks. How long was I out?"

"Two hours, give or take."

"Huh. That's more than I've gotten in a while." Her mouth twists.

"Well, I'm glad Holly Peak could provide you with the right amenities."

That gets me the grin I hoped for. "It's definitely on the rustic side. It does beat my hatchback, though."

My blood runs cold. "Hold up. You've been sleeping in your car?"

Her brow wrinkles. "Sometimes, yeah."

"Just how often are you doing that?"

"Every so often. I did it yesterday. Why?"

"Wren, are you homeless?" I can't think of any other conceivable reason she's sleeping in a car, especially during the winter.

"I mean, kind of?"

"Kind of?!"

She startles a little at the force of my words. I flex my hands, loosening the muscles I've been clenching into tight fists. It doesn't help. I still feel...tight.

"Hugo," Wren calls firmly.

The dog trots over to me, tapping my hand with his cold nose. I focus on the point of contact, tracing his snout.

"I'm safe, Nico."

I stare at the woman sitting across the cabin from me. She wasn't *safe* when she was stranded by herself on the trail, and she's not *safe* sleeping in a damn car. The only way I know for certain that she's safe is if I keep her right next to me.

"I would hobble over to you, but...ya know," she says, giving her injured leg a wiggle. "Sit."

Hugo butts my thigh with his massive head, shoving me toward the spot Wren is patting.

I don't know why she's being so welcoming all of a sudden. It's either pity for me and this obvious panic attack or leftover chill from her nap.

The cot sits lower than I factored, and I end up half-falling onto it. Thankfully, it holds up; the old metal frame is sturdy despite its age.

"You want to do that, uh, breathing thing?" Wren asks.

"Nah, I'm good now." Or I will be once she gives me some proper answers.

I feel it then, Wren's pinky finger brushing along the side of my palm. It's so subtle I would have missed it if I wasn't so damn in tune with her every move.

She tugs away, and the moment is over before it even started. But it's a sign that maybe, just maybe, she is in this with me.

"Do you want to take a turn with the bed now?"

"No, thanks."

"Any updates on the storm while I was asleep?"

"Nope."

"Ah."

"Yeah."

"Do you—"

"Want to—"

We laugh, our voices mingling together in an odd sort of harmony.

"I was going to ask if you wanted to play a game?" she says. "I don't know what kind of activities you have stashed in here."

I don't either. My life isn't compatible with playing games. "The volunteers might have left something behind."

"In that black hole of a closet?" She bites her lip on a grin, the color in her face adorable and sexy at the same time.

"Don't remind me about the closet," I say with a groan, rising from the cot and heading toward the desk in the office.

"F IND ANY GAMES OVER there?" she calls. I can hear the cot squeaking as she gets up. Her footsteps shuffle slowly toward me.

I try in vain to shove the desk drawer shut, but the damn thing is stuck, the wood straining and moaning with each push. I don't want Wren to see the contents of the drawer and get the wrong idea.

"What the fuck?" she says from over my shoulder. It's too late. She's seen it. "How much lube is in there? And is that an entire year's supply of condoms? Just what are you ski patrol freaks getting into on Holly Peak?"

My face is hot. "I did *not* know this was here. It's either a prank, or I'm gonna have to have a conversation about professional behavior with some of the volunteers because..."

She snickers, pulling the blanket she has wrapped around her shoulders tighter. "This is worse than the closet, isn't it?"

"Not. Funny. This place is going to be the death of me."

The laughter on her face falls, her skin paling.

"I'm sorry. Your dad. I didn't think."

"No, no. It;s not your fault. It's just..."

"Just what, Wren?"

"Can we just go into the other room and figure out what we're going to do? Not stand here next to a drawer full of lube and condoms?"

"You still want to play a game?"

"Did you find one?"

"Nah, but I figure we can come up with something of our own, don't you?"

"**T**WO TRUTHS AND A *lie*? Are we in middle school, Wren?"

"Well, what sort of game do you propose instead, Dominic?"

I narrow my eyes at her. Nobody calls me Dominic besides my grandmother.

"I was thinking something like *twenty questions* or *truth or dare*." Any game that would require Wren to give me some genuine answers.

She still hasn't fully explained to me how a person could be *kind of* homeless.

"Those aren't any better than my idea."

"No, but only one of those games involves you lying."

She raises a ginger brow. "And which of the two of us is the liar?"

I yield that point to her. "I thought you were over that."

Her green eyes are molten. "You can go first."

Wren might think that she's putting me at a disadvantage, but what she doesn't realize is that by letting me answer first, I get to set the tone of our game. I can give her a bullshit, basic answer about my favorite color—orange—or how many countries I've visited—a whopping two—or I can dig deep.

"Game on."

CHAPTER SEVEN

Wren

NICO LOOKS FAR TOO comfortable and excited to play this silly game. He's leaned back in one of the desk chairs with his legs propped up on the other.

I keep my distance on the cot, unsettled by the look of mischief in his eyes.

I remember that look all too well. It always led to a world of trouble.

He steeples his fingers, tapping the joined pads of his pointer fingers to his lips. I've noticed he's a tapper, and there seems to be some sort of pattern to the movements, but I can't quite catch on to it without staring invasively.

"Are you going to start?" I ask.

He lowers his hands, unveiling a smooth grin. My stomach drops. I'm not sure if it's nerves or my inconvenient attraction to Nico.

"Oh, I'm starting, alright. You know the rules of the game, don't you, Wren?"

I blink, caught up in the way his dark eyes are fixed on me, shining in the glow of the naked lightbulbs.

Is Nico flirting with me?

I shake my head. There's no way. "I know the rules," I say, the words sounding weak to my ears.

"Good. So, you won't mind if we change them up a bit?"

"I...guess not."

He may not be flirting, but he's definitely up to something.

"I propose we tell each other our truths and our lies, but we don't reveal which one is the lie until the game is over."

It sounds simple enough. "Fine. Now, quit stalling."

"Not stalling. Just making sure you're ready." He laces his hands behind his head, relaxing deeper into his makeshift recliner.

I have a sudden urge to launch something at him—hard—but the only thing I have nearby is a blanket.

I settle for a glare that only makes him chuckle under his breath.

It's a good thing I'll never have to see him again after we get out of this cabin.

"I am tired all the time," Nico's voice cuts in. I can't read his face. He's still lounging, his gaze set on the ceiling.

"Is that your first truth?" It's weak as far as truths go.

"How do you know that's not the lie?"

"I have eyes."

He clucks his tongue. "We don't know each other anymore, though, right? Maybe you're not so good at reading me."

"Keep. Going." I widen my mouth, loosening the muscles in my jaw.

"My best friend is my dog." Another obvious truth. He's bad at this game. I already know the next one is his lie.

He kicks his feet down from the chair, planting his feet firmly on the plank wood floor, his eyes squaring up with mine.

"I still think you're the most beautiful woman I've ever seen."

Something akin to pain washes over my body. I want to yell, to rage at him for putting me through this when I can't get escape.

I swallow past the lump forming in my throat, determined not to let him see.

It's my turn, and despite my insistence that Nico and I are strangers to one another, it isn't true. I know how to get to him, for good or for ill, the same way he does me.

"My favorite color is black."

He spears me with a dark look. If only he knew that my real favorite color is the exact shade of his hair, those blue-black waves mixed with streams of chestnut brown.

"I've been traveling across the country since last February spreading Dad's ashes at his favorite ski resorts and hiking trails."

Nico perks up, his left foot bouncing up and down. Hugo looks over from his spot across the room, decides we're boring, and lays back down.

Now, it's time for my lie. I suck in a bracing breath.

"I haven't missed you at all."

He doesn't react. I wonder if he knows I'm lying. He's better than I am at this fucking game, which I now realize is the exact reason he didn't mind that I picked it.

"I love my job, even if I resent it a little bit lately. I've never been happier and lonelier in a place than I have been in Holly Hill." He pauses. I watch his jaw tick. "The biggest regret of my life is the way I went off the rails after Jonno got hurt."

My head spins. I don't know what the lie is and what's real anymore. I don't know what kind of twisted play Nico is making right now. Does he hate me that much for leaving him?

I want—*need*—to tap out. "Nico, I—"

"Your turn."

"I don't think I can—"

"You *can*." He means that I have no other choice. He'll wait me out until I talk. This hurts more than support group does.

"Okay." I rub my thumbs together, avoiding Nico's knowing eyes. "Holly Peak is the last resort on my list, and I have no plan for my life afterward." *Truth*. "I had to leave college, had to leave everything behind, nine years ago because Dad had a stroke and needed a full-time caregiver." *Truth*. "And last, I really, really hate you." *Lie, lie, lie*.

Nico's face is stark and unreadable. He might as well still be wearing that damn mask. Only the constant up and down motion of his left heel tapping on the floor offers any hint of what he's feeling.

He has certainly unsettled me, left me wanting to ask him a million more questions, made me eager to unwrap him and all the mysteries I know he has buried inside of him.

The biggest lie I told tonight was when I implied that this man was shallow. There isn't, and never has been, anything shallow about him, even if he hasn't always known that himself.

Now, he won't stop looking at me, as if searching for the hidden depths within me. I'm not so sure I have anything left to give.

"Aren't you going to use your turn?" I ask.

A muscle jumps in his jaw, and he leans in. I hold my breath, waiting for his next round of obvious truths and devastating lies.

"You win."

Huh?

"What do you mean, I win?"

"I mean, I'm done with this game, Wren."

"We've barely gotten started!" I'm protesting far too much for a person who tried to beg off a few minutes ago.

He shrugs. "I'm done."

"B—but, don't you want to find out what was real, or fake, or—"

"Wren. It's finished."

So flat and final, like a straightaway with no surprises. Is that what this newer, more settled version of Nico needs these days?

I huff, half-turning away on the little cot. "I see what you're doing."

"Yeah, what's that?"

I sneak a peek to find him tilted back in his chair again, his head tipped toward the ceiling and his eyes pinched shut. His Adam's apple bobs in his throat.

"Chickening out. You agreed to play, and now you're just...quitting," I say, my body taut as I wait for his reaction. I can almost predict his response. Something about how judging him for quitting on a commitment is ironic coming from me.

He stretches his neck, turning his head slowly from side to side. "If you're trying to get a rise out of me, you're barking up the wrong tree. I just don't feel like playing anymore."

Why am I so disappointed when this is only going to hurt me?

Maybe it's like what we've talked about in support group: that getting close to someone, loving someone, carries inherent vulnerability.

Being around Nico feels a lot like when I first started skiing again last February. Painful and uncomfortable, like being stretched and rotated a touch past the point of comfort.

But afterward, I was lighter. My heart was full and my head clear. I soon got used to the pain and sore muscles until going too long without hiking or skiing felt wrong.

Dad was always pushing for me to live more, to push myself past fear, and to leave him alone for longer periods of time. He would have been proud of the way I've gotten back into it over the last few months.

My fingers itch. I reach for a pocket that isn't there.

"Can I have my jacket?" I say through numb lips.

That appears to affect him more than my needling did. He lifts his head, the lines in his forehead crinkling.

"Are you cold?" He looks behind him. "I'll add more wood to the stove. Hold on—"

"Nico. I'm not cold. Just give me my jacket."

He stands, and although the concerned look hasn't gone from his face, he brings the jacket to me.

I snatch it from his hands, fumbling with the fabric until I reach the interior pocket.

It's still there, not that I thought it wasn't. But knowing it's there, a piece of Dad, is reassuring.

"Is that..."

"A bag of my dad's ashes, yeah."

"What are you..."

I glance up from the small plastic bag and its contents. "Are you going to complete a sentence? Or maybe it's another symptom of your 'quitting halfway through' disease."

He gives me no reaction, and I want to scream. I prefer Nico being mad at me to this...ultra-chill, non-caring facade of his.

"I was just going to ask what you plan on doing with them."

I nod. If he's willing to have a civil conversation, I can dial it back too. "I only have a little left, see?" I hold the clear bag aloft. "I divided up the ashes, one bag for each resort and park I wanted to hit. One bag left and then...I'm done, I guess."

"You said you...don't know what you'll do after."

I raise an eyebrow. "How do you know that wasn't the lie?"

"I guess I don't know."

I sigh. "It wasn't—the lie, that is. I've been pretty nomadic, I suppose you could say, over the last few months. I sold Dad's house, quit my boring remote job, put a bunch of things in storage, and this has been my life ever since."

"Just you, your dad—kind of—and the great outdoors."

"Yeah."

"That sounds..."

Yet another unfinished sentence. He doesn't need to complete it, though. "Lonely, yes."

I smile ruefully.

"I know the feeling," he says.

"Oh, so the happy-but-lonely dichotomy you feel in Holly Hill was your truth?"

He laughs, just a little. "It was. Not that you didn't know that already."

"You've got Hugo, at least."

"He's a pretty solid companion."

"I'm glad you have him. Someone to love." Nico was always good at giving love.

He gives me a look I can't interpret. "Me too. We're lucky, me and him."

Another shrill whistle of wind cuts through the cabin, cooling the room in an instant. Nico groans. "I'm gonna need to bring more wood in for the stove."

I glance out the window at the wall of white flurries. "Are you sure?" I don't envy his going out there.

"I'm sure. Unless you want your toes to freeze off."

"That does not sound like fun, no."

The corners of his eyes crinkle. He rises from his chair. "I'll be right—"

"Nico, wait!"

I'm suddenly struck with terror at the idea of him going back out into the storm, of getting lost in the blizzard, and leaving me here alone.

He pauses in donning his red ski patrol jacket. "Yeah?"

"I, um..." I worry the plastic bag between my fingers, letting the material slip and slide over my skin.

He shifts his weight. "I can't let it get too cold in here, Wren. I'm sorry. Say what you need to say, and say it quick."

He slips his face covering over his head before zipping the jacket up the rest of the way. It's fascinating to watch him put his armor on.

"Wren?"

"I'm sorry!" The words spill out of me, overflowing past my lips.

His heavy brow comes down. "For what?"

"For leaving. Back then. Without telling you." I swipe the pad of my finger under my eye, and it comes away suspiciously damp.

He's white-knuckling his beanie and goggles, his grip so fierce I can feel it from across the cabin.

"You're bringing this up now?" His beautiful voice is gruff and muffled, as if he's already back under his mask.

"I just...please be careful out there."

He tosses the goggles to the floor and stalks over to where I'm perched on the edge of the cot, wrapped in my blanket shield.

Without speaking, he drops to a crouch, not unlike the position he was in when he was examining my ankle.

He takes a single finger and tips my chin up until I meet his eyes.

"We are going to talk when I get back inside."

"I know," I whisper.

He shifts his head down in a swift nod before standing up, his finger slipping away.

"Good. Because, Wren?"

"Yeah?"

"That game we played? Those lies I told?"

As if I could forget.

"They were all truths."

I'm breathless when he slips out the door, a gust of wind and snow carrying him into an endless sea of white.

CHAPTER EIGHT

Wren

M Y HEAD, MUCH LIKE the landscape, is swirling when Nico returns with an armful of split wood. He was gone less than five minutes, according to my watch, but it felt far longer.

He kicks the door open, a stack of wood spilling from his arms. He sets that stack down, then leans out the door to gather two more before finally closing off our cozy cabin the storm.

I clear my throat. "You didn't have to cut all that, did you?" I have to admit that, even amid a blizzard, Nico chopping wood makes for an appealing visual.

He tugs his face covering down over his neck to reveal a smirk. He knows exactly where my mind was headed. "I'd have to be the fastest chopper known to man for that. We keep stacks of wood around the back of the cabin. This should be enough for the rest of the night, I hope."

The large pile of logs is another reminder of how long Nico and I will be stuck inside this cabin together. Another reminder that I can't run away or hide from my emotions.

A blast of heat warms my face as Nico finishes up at the stove. I watch through sleepy eyes as he moves to the tall cupboard where he got our snacks earlier.

"Want some?" he asks.

I open my heavy lids to find him holding up a handful of tiny liquor bottles, his fingers wrapped tightly around the slim necks.

"A true après-ski. Are you allowed to drink on the job?" I tease, taking a cinnamon-flavored whiskey from his grasp.

He laughs, lowering his narrow hips into his uncomfortable-looking desk chair. The wheels groan, and one arm tilts down, hanging in a lopsided fashion.

"It's not a twenty-four seven gig. I'm only on shift when the trails are open, and well..."

"So, you're making an exception for me, then." I twist the top off the whiskey.

He eyes me over the neck of his own miniature bottle, though his is cheap tequila.

"In more ways than one."

My cheeks warm under his gaze.

We're definitely flirting. It's heady and weird and confusing. Perhaps our forced proximity has us speed-running through every emotional beat under the sun to get us to...wherever we end up.

Going our separate ways, more than likely. I sip my whiskey, regretting my choice not to down it in a single shot.

"So," I say, letting the word linger in the air.

He smiles. "So."

He's so annoying. I finish the rest of the whiskey, motioning to Nico for another with a flick of my fingers.

He obliges, passing me a tequila bottle that matches his own. We toast, a dull, plasticky tap, before draining the contents of our bottles in swift gulps.

I shiver, the alcohol rushing through my bloodstream. "I can't remember the last time I drank."

"No? I'll put them away." He reaches down to gather the small collection of bottles he's set on the floor. His desk chair wobbles.

"Sorry," he says, as if he's in any way responsible for the state of the chair.

Maybe he is. I bet he's the one in charge of ordering needed supplies, ski patrol desk chairs included.

"You can sit here." I scoot over, closer to the small pillow I used during my brief nap. "And don't worry about putting the booze away. It's fine."

"You sure?" he asks. I get the sense he has included both of my statements in that query.

"I'm sure. I'm not against alcohol or anything. I've just never been much for drinking outside social occasions, and those have been few and far between."

He lowers himself down to sit at the foot of the cot. "Yeah, I get that. I kinda figured it might help...relax us a little before we have that conversation."

I look over at him and smile. "It was a good idea."

"One more each? So we don't overdo it and I end up skiing with a hangover tomorrow?"

"Wouldn't be the first time," I say, holding my palm flat for the mini vodka bottle.

"Here goes."

✿ ✿ ✿ ✿ ✿ ✿ ✿

M Y BELLY IS WARM and my limbs loose for the first time in ages, since even before Dad died.

Was getting drunk the key to all my problems this entire time?

I look at Nico, settled on the opposite edge of the old cot.

It's not the alcohol. It's him.

If only this could last beyond tonight and outside the walls of this cabin.

"When did you find out your dad had a stroke?"

I clear my throat. We've hit our self-imposed limit of three mini-bottles each. I'm tempted to drink another, but it would be pointless. There isn't enough liquid courage in the world to make this story a fun one to tell.

I finger the edge of the navy-blue sleeping bag. "Not long after we went on that hike in the state park. The one—"

He tips his head back and groans. "Yeah, I remember the one. God, you were so fucking mad at me that day."

My laugh is sticky. "So mad. Like, I was tempted to shove you off the trail and down that gorge, I think."

He gives me a sideways glance. "I wouldn't have needed much help to fall, considering all the stupid shit I was doing. Walking on the trail edge, ignoring all the markers. Man, I was an asshole, wasn't I?"

"Pretty much, yeah."

"It wasn't just that day either."

I swallow. "No. It wasn't just that day."

Nico's wild streak had started months before that.

"I'm sorry. Jonno got hurt and...I just didn't know how to deal. It was like I went searching for danger just to prove I could conquer it. Looking back on it now, I don't even recognize that kid."

"I don't know if he would recognize you either. Do you still see..."

"Jonno? Yeah, every once in a while. He started skiing again, actually." Nico's friend, who soon became our mutual friend, had loved skiing before a skiing accident where he'd endured a fairly significant concussion.

My eyes widen. "Really? He seemed pretty dead set on avoiding it the last time I saw him." Granted, that was nine years ago. People change, and I've missed nearly all of it.

"He was. Didn't want to risk another head injury, but he came out to visit me the year before last. We took things slow. He got me to try snowshoeing."

I snicker. Nico always used to say the activity looked lame and boring, especially compared to skiing. "That sounds really great."

"It was cool, yeah."

"Did he or the others... Did they ever..."

"They asked about you. Wondered where you went. Why your phone was off. And then after a bit...they stopped."

It's what I'm expecting, so much so that I'm shocked when it hurts.

"It was wrong of me to leave like that." Not only did I hurt Nico, I hurt our friends too. I didn't just leave *him*. I left *everyone* behind.

He nods slowly. "It was. But I was wrong too. I was acting like an overgrown toddler. You couldn't count on me. I get why you left."

"I don't want you to go easy on me, okay? I could have...I don't know, talked to you about how I felt. At least told you I was ending things instead of just..."

"Leaving me a note on a Scooby Doo notepad that said 'I can't do this anymore,' changing your number, and disappearing into the night?"

"Wow, nineteen-year-old Wren fucking sucked, huh?"

"I still have flashbacks when I hear the Scooby Doo theme song."

A laugh bubbles up from deep within my gut. Hugo raises his head at the sound, his jowls twitching.

"Is it cool to joke about flashbacks when you have actual PTSD?"

He smiles. "Only if I do it."

"How did you get into the wildland firefighting stuff anyway?"

"A guy I met in one of my classes was doing it. It had been about two years since you left, and I was pretty lost. Still taking dumb risks, not caring if I got hurt or worse. I figured, at least if I get hurt doing this, it's for a good cause."

"Did you ever...get hurt?"

The corner of his lips tilts up. "Not me. But...others did. People who did care if they got injured, or who had other people who cared. That's the part that fucked me up the most."

"But this time...this time you're not..."

"This time I'm handling it differently."

He is, and in a way that I can't help but be envious of. He's retained those shades of Dom, but Nico is steady, and composed, and reliable.

He's who I needed nine years ago. He just hadn't gotten there yet.

"I'm not handling things well," I say. The confession spills out, harsher on my throat than that first shot of cinnamon whiskey.

Nico stands from his spot at the other end of the cot. My heart plummets. He's leaving.

Only he doesn't leave, because he's not afraid of big emotions anymore like he used to be. Not like how I was nine years ago.

Not like I still am now.

His long body melts down until he is sitting on his heels between my bent knees. Those beautiful, tanned hands take hold of my face on either side, cradling it like something precious.

He did say he wasn't lying when he told me I was still the most beautiful woman he'd ever seen. It's only when I feel his fingers shaking that I believe him.

"Will you tell me about your life, Wren? No games, no negotiations, no alcohol, just...talk to me. Please?"

It's the easiest *yes* I've ever given.

CHAPTER NINE

Nico

I 'VE BEEN WAITING TO hear Wren tell me she's sorry for leaving me since the day she left. I used to lie in my bed and imagine it, how her lips would form the words, and how I would stare blankly at her before turning my back and walking away.

The reality is a far cry from what I pictured as a young, dumb, impulsive kid. And turning away from her isn't an option I'm willing to consider. Nineteen-year-old Wren might have sucked, but so did twenty-year-old Nico.

Neither of us are kids anymore.

There's a tiny, reddish-brown eyelash just under the shadow of her left eye. Her lids flutter closed as I lean in and blow gently, letting the lash float away on the breath. Her mouth curves in a tremulous smile.

If someone had asked me last year, or ten years ago, I would have said it was impossible for me to want Wren more than I did the moment I saw her in her ugly ski pants. But somehow, in this precise moment, I want this grown-up, struggling-but-trying version of Wren more than I've ever wanted anything before in my life.

We have a mountain of baggage to sort through, and she's still wearing those hideous ski pants.

"I'm surprised you never got rid of these," I say, fingering the material.

Her smile firms. "I like abstract art."

I rise to my knees and press my lips to hers. It's impulsive, sure. I might be Nico now, but I've still got a bit of Dom in me.

And I can't spend another second of my life *not* kissing Wren.

Lips hit teeth, and I know she's still smiling. I pull back enough to catch her eye.

She nods, enough for me to know this...us...is right.

I kiss her again. Her lips open under mine, and she tastes better than I remember. Cool and icy with a blast of cinnamon whiskey that sets me on fire.

Her small hands come to my shoulders, a silent cue to get closer.

I waste no time, placing a flat palm on the center of her chest to gently press her back on the cot, following her down with one knee then the other on either side of her legs. Our tongues tangle, warm and smooth. Wren's fingers pull the small hairs at the nape of my neck in a tight grip as her hips jog against mine, desperate and looking for friction.

My chest fills. No one has taken care of Wren—sexually or otherwise—in a long time. I'm going to take care of her, starting right fucking now.

I trail open-mouthed kisses under her chin, across her cheek, below her ear, rolling each freckle under my tongue, savoring the taste I've been craving for too damn long.

The neckline of her shirt is in the way. I stretch the pink fabric as far as it can go as I lick down, down, down.

"Nico, wait." Her gasp cuts through. I force myself to lift my head.

Fuck that, I want to say. But I'm not totally insane.

"Want me to stop?" I can hardly breathe, and she wants me to *wait*. I've been waiting for nine years.

"No!"

Thank G od. I lower my head, nipping the rolling line of her collarbone as punishment.

"Don't want you to...stop. But. Don't we need to...talk?"

"Yep," I say, returning to her mouth, licking inside those pretty pink lips, our kisses punctuated by breathy words and sighs. "Later."

"Okay."

"Good."

"This feels..."

"Better."

"Yeah."

Wren's slightly chilled hands find their way up under my fleece pullover and t-shirt.

Meanwhile, I'm still tugging at the neckline of her shirt. It needs to come off. I need more of that warm, freckled skin pressed to mine.

She sits up, causing me to scoot back a fraction, then glares in the face of my obvious confusion.

"Off," she says, tugging at the hem of my pullover.

I smirk. "I'll show you mine if you show me yours."

She doesn't smile, but I can tell she wants to. At heart, I'm still that punk kid she fell in love with way back when.

We remove each other's shirts, hand over hand. It's a tangled dance of limbs and frenzied determination.

We fall back into one another, our lips drawn together like magnets.

Circumstances kept Wren and me apart for nearly a decade. Less than one day in arm's reach of her, and I already can't resist.

My fingers are on her ribs, inching their way toward the thick band of her coral-colored sports bra, when Hugo barks.

It must be the second or third time he's done it, based on how impatient he sounds.

But I'm not going to stop kissing Wren. I can't stop kissing her when I've only just gotten started again. We have a hell of a lot of lost time to make up for.

Wren is the one to pull back, having enough sense for the both of us.

Her tap on my shoulder is no less urgent than my dog's barking.

I can't catch a fucking break today.

"Nico, I think he's trying to tell you something."

I groan, letting my head drop into the soft place where her neck meets her shoulder. My favorite place.

"Too nice. Can't move."

Wren lets out an uncharacteristic giggle. "I don't think you have a choice if you want him to stop barking."

Hugo trots over to the cot and nudges me in the hip with his enormous head.

The electronic shrill emanating from my jacket pocket finally registers. My cell phone. The one I'd almost forgotten I had. I was so caught up in Wren that I didn't even hear the damn thing.

I force myself off the cot, practically falling on my ass when I misjudge the short distance to the floor. I scramble up, slipping in my thick socks as I move toward the phone.

By the time I reach it, I'm panting. I have enough time to register that it's Shan, calling from her own cell.

"You good?" she asks when I finally answer.

"Never better." I was only about to fuck my ex-girlfriend in the middle of a snowstorm at my place of employment. Nothing at all of note.

"Well, I wanted to see if you still have electric up there. The power is out down the hill."

I look around, and damn if Shan isn't right. There's still a flicker of daylight filtering through the few small windows of the cabin, but the overhead lightbulbs scattered across the ceiling have all gone out.

"Power is out for us too."

I hear Wren's soft intake of breath behind me. She hadn't noticed our predicament either. I press the button on the screen to put the call on speaker, wanting to keep her in the loop.

"We will be fine," I say over my shoulder. She's gingerly shuffling over, her upper body wrapped in a blanket.

"Is that the crazy skier who decided to go out in the middle of a snowstorm?" Shan asks, the excitement clear in her voice.

I grit my teeth. "Her name is *Wren*."

"Hey, I'm not saying anything different from what you were mumbling under your breath when you and Hugo were suiting up to find her."

Holy fuck. This is the last thing I need when all I want to do is go back to taking off Wren's clothes.

"Hi, Shan. It's good to meet you," Wren interjects.

I whip my head toward her. She's being *friendly*. At least she's not bothered by hearing that I was bitching about going out in the storm earlier.

"Hi, Wren! I hope you don't mind us calling you crazy, but..."

"The boot fits."

"Exactly! Now, make sure this guy shows you where we keep the—"

"Go home, Shan."

"Sorry. Can't do that. Travel ban, remember? I am going to be right here, all night, my dulcet tones keeping you and crazy-ass Wren company. How about that?"

Absolutely fucking not. "What you should be doing is helping the resort staff take care of the guests during the power outage."

"Lame. The grounds crew is working on getting a generator going. Sadly, it won't have enough juice to give the two of you powered up again. I've been told to sit tight. Apparently, I get in the way or something."

"I can't imagine why anyone would think that."

Wren snickers, and I can't help stealing a glance. Her face is flushed and her lips slightly swollen.

"Don't tell me you're laughing at this guy's jokes, Wren," Shan cuts in. "And here I thought you were on my side. Wait...Wren. *Wren.* Nico, wasn't your—"

"Bye, Shan!" I yell over her lingering words, hanging up the phone before she embarrasses me further.

I turn toward Wren, clocking the lingering curiosity in her eyes. Shan is the nearest thing I have to a friend in Holly Hill, and hearing her and Wren hit it off so well over that call has me imagining a future that's far too early in this reconnection to imagine.

"She seems cool."

"Shan?" I say, like I don't know exactly who Wren is talking about. "When she's not being so damn annoying, she is."

"It's nice that you have someone to look out for you, Nico."

I nod. "Who looks out for you, Wren?"

She pales, but she doesn't run away this time. "I look out for myself. Always have."

Not always. Not for one blissful year before our friend got hurt, and I started acting like a child with nothing to lose. It's no wonder Wren cut me loose when things in her life took a serious turn.

"Was Shan..." Wren starts before trailing off. "What did she mean at the end there? It was like she knew my name."

I should have ended that call sooner than I did. Or never put it on speakerphone at all. But Wren and I have decided that we are being real with one another, and I won't go back on that now.

"She does know your name. Because I've talked about you—kind of a lot."

"Oh."

I laugh because I have no idea what else to do with that response. "Is that weird? Do you ever talk to people about me?"

"I think you drastically overestimate how much I talk to *anyone* at all about *anything*. I've been driving across the country with only myself for company for the better part of the year."

"The homeless thing, right?"

"Can we, uh, sit down for this, maybe?"

"Might as well."

CHAPTER TEN

Wren

I CONVINCE NICO TO grab us each another plate of snacks from the cupboard. We need fuel for the conversation we're about to have, and based on the position of the setting sun, it's going to get very dark in this cabin very soon.

Now, our plates empty, we're facing each other side by side in this cot, huddled close in a single sleeping bag. I'm down to my sports bra and black leggings, my colorful ski pants now part of Hugo's makeshift bed. Nico is wearing a pair of merino wool long johns and nothing else. The room is cast in long shadows. It should be cold, but I'm so very, very warm.

"So, yeah, I've been on this mission for Dad. He didn't ask me to do it, but it's been amazing to get back into skiing and hiking. My life was so consumed with Dad for so long—making sure he took his medicine, taking care of the house, going to all the appointments. This thing with the ashes has given me a purpose again."

"You really didn't ski at all after you left Colorado?"

I shake my head. "Nope. I didn't have the time or the energy. Dad would encourage me to get back out there, try to hype me up for it, but I couldn't leave him for that long, and he knew that too."

"I just...you were all about skiing back then. It's hard to picture you doing anything else."

"We both changed a lot, Nico. It's been a long time."

He reaches a tentative hand up to my face, smoothing back an errant piece of hair. "It almost feels like we've switched places from who we were before."

I know what he means. "A little. Dom would have *absolutely* supported me in skiing all alone in the middle of a snowstorm."

"And Nico wants to hide your skis so you never do that again."

"Oh my God, do you remember when I did that to you that first week after Jonno fell? My heart was in the right place, but the execution...yikes."

"A solid conversation would have served us well, huh?"

"We were kids. We tried our best."

"Yeah, I guess we did, in our way. But now..."

I study his face, the one that's glowing in the embers of our fire. The one that's so achingly familiar. "Now what?"

"Do you think this could work...again?"

I swallow. He's giving voice to a hope I buried long ago, so deep down I haven't allowed myself to speak about Nico or our past for years. He's talked about me to his friend, and I know it's because he's missed me—missed us.

I've avoided talking about him for the same reason. Thinking about Nico and speaking his name, whatever name he uses, hurt too much if I couldn't be with him. Even though he let me down before, no one has ever measured up to him.

"I don't know," I whisper honestly.

His eyes shutter.

"But I *want* it to work again," I continue in a rush. "I want it so badly."

Nico reaches around and grabs hold of the nape of my neck, his fingers strong and warm. "Don't say things you don't mean, Wren. Please. I've spent nine years of my life missing you, being angry with you for taking yourself away from me, and now you're somehow here, in front of me."

"I mean it. I—I don't know what I'm doing with my life, with my future after this, Nico. I can't make any promises. But I promise that I want to be with you tonight."

"If that's all you can give me, then I'm taking it."

And take it he does, his mouth coming down hard on mine.

His tongue sweeps in, and I meet it with my own. Every nerve ending in my body fires, an explosion of sparks.

We're already pressed together, and the stiff length of Nico's cock is heavy against the side of my thigh, too far from where I need him. I shift my lower leg, careful of my twisted ankle, up over his shin. He takes a hand, gripping the back of my thigh, and hitches my leg fully over his hip.

"Fuck," he says into my mouth as he notches in just right. Two thin layers of fabric are all that separate the head of his cock from my wet center.

I thrust toward him, feeling his tip nudge my opening, so close yet still so far.

Without warning, he reaches down with both hands and pushes my hips back.

"Why," I whine.

"Baby, if you keep that up, I'm gonna come in these pants, and the night will be over before it gets started."

"Just let me indulge my curiosity real quick. Find out if you still feel perfect inside me."

One of those hands moves across my hip and down between my legs until he's cupping me...right *there*. I fight the urge to twitch my hips, knowing it'll only annoy him enough to delay my gratification.

"It's cute that you think this will be quick."

He drags the pad of his finger along the center seam of my leggings, pausing at the top before tracing that same damnable line again. "If all you're willing to give me is one night, I'm going to take my time. I'm going to savor you. I'm going to drink in every last sound you make. And when I finally fill you up, there will be no question about just how perfect my dick feels inside of you."

My universe boils down to his finger between my thighs as he drags it along my center once more before placing just the right amount of pressure on my clit.

I come hard and fast, the orgasm hitting me like an avalanche.

"Oh my God," I say, scrunching my eyes shut.

"Don't be shy, Wren. That was sexy as hell."

I bite my lip, forcing myself to look at him. His dark hair is rumpled, and his pupils are wide and so black I could get sucked into them forever. His lips are shiny, and the tip of his tongue peeks out from behind his teeth.

"It's been a while."

More like years.

"For me too."

"Yeah?"

"Yeah. And it was worth every bit of the wait. You're fucking gorgeous."

He catches the lobe of my ear in his teeth, and I shiver. I feel the stiff press of his cock against me again, and already the orgasm I just had isn't enough.

I smooth my hands over Nico's shoulders, down the broad expanse of his chest, and toward the waistband of his pants. I run a single finger along the elastic edge while I lower the other hand down, down, down, until I reach my destination.

I barely grab hold of his cock when he tugs my wrist away, up and over our heads.

"No, no, no. I'm getting another one out of you before I let you touch me."

I moan, free and unashamed at how much I want him. If going off like a rocket after hardly a touch from him served one purpose, it was to take the pressure off.

"Do it, then."

He smirks, and I've got him exactly where I want him.

He dips his head into the opening of the sleeping bag, kissing under my chin, over my collarbone, and across my chest. He hits the fabric of my sports bra, the material too tight for him to wedge a finger beneath it.

My back bows as he demonstrates his dissatisfaction with my underwear choices with a sharp bite to the stiff peak of my nipple. He consoles me by giving it a lick, letting his tongue wet the cloth before sucking it inside.

He repeats the move on the opposite nipple before raising his head to look at me. His head is partially obscured by the sleeping bag, all but his eyes in shadow.

"Nico," I say.

"Wren."

"This...you..."

"Yeah," he says, rising in a smooth motion to kiss me again, our mouths and lips a tangle of need.

My belly goes concave as Nico slides his hand down into the waistband of my leggings. He smiles into our kiss when his middle finger parts the seam of my pussy, dipping inside the wet heat at my core.

We groan in unison as that long, thick finger sinks in to the third knuckle, sliding in with ease.

"God, you feel good," he says as my world shrinks to only his hand. "You're squeezing the life out of this finger right now. Think you can take another one?"

I nod, frantic and desperate for what his words promise.

He takes his time, a slow, delicious stretch as my body adjusts to a second, then a third digit. He pumps me a few times before my hips take over, and I'm fucking his hand with abandon. The cot rocks, dragging and creaking across the wood floor.

"That's it, baby. Ride my hand. You're so fucking wet. Give me just one more, and then you'll get this dick."

His dirty words in that sexy voice, the wet sounds of him thrusting in and out of me, and the sheer beauty of Nico overload my senses. My interior muscles spasm, pulsing around Nico's fingers as my second orgasm hits.

"Fuck yes," Nico says, the satisfaction clear in his voice. He's cocky, but I suppose he has every right to be right now.

He pulls his hand out of my pants, and I feel the dampness on his fingers as he drags it up my stomach. I watch, feeling the buildup of a third orgasm as he lifts his hand to his mouth and sucks each of his fingers, one by one.

"If you don't get up right now and get one of those condoms..."

He slides out of the sleeping bag and across the room faster than I've seen him move yet. Hugo, still passed out on the floor, lets out a loud snore, oblivious to the wicked chaos going on in the cabin.

Nico is back at the cot in a flash, where he pauses at the head of our makeshift bed. I hold his gaze as he lowers his pants, inch by inch, past the taut ridges of muscles along his waist, until his hard cock is on display.

I have no shame in watching as he bends a little to get the pants all the way down, straightening up once he's completely bared. He opens the condom wrapper with his teeth then rolls the thin latex down over his erection. His brow wrinkles in concentration, and I'm immediately transported back to the first time I saw him do this with that same focused look on his face.

He looks the same but different. There's a new scar that runs along his muscled obliques. The silhouette of burning evergreens tattooed on his thigh that I've never seen before.

I worry my lip between my teeth as he steps closer.

"Like what you see?" he asks.

"Cocky, much?"

He snickers. "Only with you."

"Then yeah, I like it."

He grins, a wicked flash of teeth, as he leans down to capture my mouth with his.

I laugh as he slides his way back into our sleeping bag, our limbs tangled and twisted.

But then he's there, done with the teasing, thrusting in until he's buried to the hilt. I can't laugh any longer because I'm too busy gasping.

The cot moves across the cabin floor, and the sleeping bag constricts our movements, but I don't mind. I don't think Nico does either, what with the way he tosses his head back and groans with each thrust.

Nico and I always did our best work in awkward positions. Tiny dorm room twin beds. A dingy hotel bathroom when we shared a room with Jonno and his girlfriend on a ski trip. A tent in the middle of a busy campsite, me biting the palm of his hand to keep quiet when I came.

Tonight, I can be as loud as I want. It's only us and the storm to drown out our cries.

We kiss and kiss until I'm panting, breathing so hard I can't keep up. Nico buries his face in my neck, kissing and licking and sucking along the delicate skin there.

My back arches, changing the angle of our hips. We both moan as Nico somehow gets deeper, each thrust putting more and more pressure on my clit.

"Come for me, Wren," he orders, not sounding remotely out of breath. The only sign he's at all affected is his now-stuttering rhythm as my pussy clenches around him. Somehow, he's got more stamina and endurance than he did as a teenager. It would infuriate me if I weren't the lucky beneficiary of said stamina.

I reach for his head, cupping the back of it and bringing his lips to mine. My fingernails are in his scalp and his tongue in my mouth when I come again, Nico not far behind.

He falls down onto me, letting me feel his weight before he starts to shift himself off.

"Stay," I say, gripping his shoulder with my fingertips. It's cozy this way, like I'm safe and surrounded inside our little sleeping bag in this warm, dark cabin.

"I'm too heavy."

"You're warm. I haven't been warm in so long." My words slur, and I can hardly keep my eyes open.

"Let me just take care of this condom. Be right back." He rolls away but not before taking my face in his hands and pressing a soft kiss to my forehead. My eyes flutter closed, and all I can think is, *when did I get so soft?*

CHAPTER ELEVEN

Nico

IT'S MORNING, AND MY time with Wren wasn't a dream. She is real, and she is here, and I think she might be mine again.

If only I can convince her to stay.

I may be halfway there if the way she's clinging to me is anything to go by. Not that we have much room to maneuver in this sleeping bag, but Wren is sleeping basically on top of me, her hand pressed to my chest and her head in the crook of my arm. I exhale lightly, blowing away a stray strand of her hair that's tickling my cheek.

My back and neck are killing me after sleeping on the old cot, my stomach feels like it's eating itself, and I can't wait to drink some real coffee.

It was still the best night of sleep I've had in ages.

Maybe even in nine years.

I hear the familiar interruption of my radio. Wren mumbles before opening her big green eyes.

"Do you have to get up and get that?"

"Unfortunately, I do."

"Can you just wait"—she lifts her head up the tiniest bit and kisses me—"one more second." Another small kiss.

When she goes to pull back, I cup the back of her neck, keeping her close.

We're both breathing hard when there's more noise from the radio.

"Fuck me." Wren giggles as I grumble and slip out from our cozy cocoon.

"What, Shan?"

"Some greeting, sunshine. Storm's over. Thought you and Wrenny Poo might like to know. Should be smooth skiing back down to the lodge. Travel ban has lifted too, in case you'd like to sleep in a proper bed."

I look out the window to see that Shan is right. Clear skies and morning sunshine.

I find I'm not in any rush to get back to civilization, though.

"I'm gonna have to work the trails today, aren't I?" *Please say no, please say no.* I love my job—I do—but there are more pressing things I need to deal with first.

"No, sir." *Thank fuck.* "Boss man caved and approved overtime for you for last night. Guess it's bad PR not to recognize the hard work of ski patrol during a weather emergency. Volunteers are showing up in droves today."

"Because none of them got any skiing in yesterday."

"Hey, I don't question the motive if the outcome is to my liking. Now, get your ass down the mountain so I can meet the mysterious Wren."

I peer over my shoulder to see that Wren is no longer in the room. The door to the small bathroom is closed, so thankfully she didn't hear Shan's comment. I don't like the thought of her feeling pressured.

I'm not sure that Wren wants the same thing that I do. I want her here with me in Holly Hill, side by side, for as long as she's willing to tolerate me. But the only thing Wren committed to was one night. And like a starving man, I agreed to that.

The muscles in my jaw clench. "About that..." I say to Shan.

"Why are you saying it like that? Do you not want Wren to know that your best friend in this town is a crazy person? She's crazy too, remember?!"

I press my fingertips into my temples. "Again, Shan, with the radio channel."

"Oh, psh. I don't care who hears me. If this Wren isn't ready to meet me, that's okay. Just make sure to remind her that I've been waiting to meet the woman my friend has been talking about for the last five years, and I'm not above a guilt trip."

"Goodbye, Shannon." I turn the volume knob on the radio all the way down.

There is a tough conversation that Wren and I need to have this morning. But when the bathroom door pops open, and she hits me with a soft, post-sleep smile, I can't bear the thought of ruining that.

If Wren doesn't want the same thing that I do, I don't know what I'll do. It was hard enough surviving the loss of her when she disappeared the first time. I'm not so sure my heart and mind can take doing it again.

Hugo trots over to her, nosing at her hand until she starts rubbing him. I stare, drinking in the sight of this woman with my dog.

They look right together, Wren grinning and Hugo gazing up at her with a dopey expression on his face.

Wren glances up, tilting her head to the side in silent question.

"Shan said we should be safe to head back to the lodge now."

"Okay."

"How's the ankle feel?"

She gives it a slow wiggle, causing my heart rate to soar. "Not bad. Probably not up to skiing my way down the trail, though."

"It's fine. That's why I've got the toboggan."

She bends at the waist, getting her face close to the dog's. She's whispering something to him—something I can't quite make out.

"You trying to steal my dog, Wren?"

"Maybe. I could use a friend like him, I think."

"You could, uh, hang out with him as much as you want," I say, testing the waters.

She doesn't reply, instead grasping Hugo's head in her hands, placing a kiss between his ears before straightening.

"Should we get dressed?"

We're still in our inner layers, my uniform scattered across the cabin floor and her bright ski pants and pink shirt layered atop one of the rolling desk chairs near the cot.

"Guess so."

Wren makes quick work of dressing while I tidy up the worst of the mess in the cabin. I'll have to come back in a few days to do a more thorough cleanup. Some volunteers will have to come with me so I can show them the correct way to organize the supply closet.

"Don't put your boot on too tight," I tell Wren as I slip on each layer of clothing. I'm fastening the chin strap of my helmet and sliding my goggles into place before she finishes.

"You're fast," she comments.

"Lots of practice," I say, crouching low to buckle Hugo's vest.

I walk to the door, studying Wren as she takes one last look around the cabin.

"It feels weird to leave," she says.

"Does it?" I want to pry, but I can't keep leading her to the vulnerability point. I have to let her come to me if I ever hope to keep her here.

"Yeah. We've been in our own little world, tucked away where no one can find us. Facing the real world is...daunting."

"Any ideas on what you're going to do after this? After you leave your dad here?"

She shrugs then looks me head-on. "I have no idea."

"Would you ever consider staying? Here in Holly Hill?" *With me?*

Her mouth drops open the tiniest bit before she slams it shut again. "I—I can't answer that question, Nico."

"Will you ever be able to answer it? Or are you planning on disappearing on me again?"

"I won't disappear. I'm past that, just like you're past your reckless stage."

"Fine, but what will you do, Wren? Live in your car forever, no job, no family, nothing?"

Her lips are a straight line, and I've pushed too far too fast. "Thanks for that stunning description of my life and my prospects, Dom."

I throw my hands up. Hugo whines. "I'm sorry. I didn't mean it like that. But I'm worried."

Her throat bobs. "You need to give me some time to figure things out."

"How much time?" I decided a split second after I saw her with Hugo on the trail. Her hesitancy gnaws at the muscle deep in my chest.

"Until the bottom of the mountain, at the very least."

That, I can give her.

Chapter Twelve

Wren

T HE LAST OF DAD'S ashes slips from the plastic bag as the ski patrol sled hits a rut in the snow. My stomach dips.

I've finished my mission—the one Dad didn't send me on but that was in his honor all the same.

It's given me purpose again after losing him. I thought I would be at cross-purposes once things were done, but I feel strangely at peace. Doing this has brought me closer to my father. It's brought me back to skiing.

And it's somehow, miraculously, brought me back to Nico.

He's been quiet on the trail, giving me the time I asked for. I swallow as I take in the straight lines of his back in his red jacket. Hugo lopes along, kicking up piles of snow alongside me.

If I could have, I would have stayed in that cabin with the two of them forever. It's the world apart from that place that scares me.

Even though I'm content now, what do I have to offer Nico and Hugo and Holly Hill?

I've been sitting still, in perpetual stasis, for nine years of my life. Can I handle settling down again?

Nico pulls up on the horns of the toboggan as we glide up to the lodge. I hadn't given it much of my attention when I arrived in a rush yesterday, but the place is beautiful.

The building is made of wood, with rising spires and a small tower to one side. It's a perfect winter castle, fitting for my knight and his trusty steed.

"What's got you smiling like that?" Nico asks, pulling my attention away from the Holly Peak lodge.

I gesture. "It's pretty."

His mouth quirks. "Here I was worried you were just happy to be rid of me."

He says it like a joke, but there's an undercurrent there, one I recognize well in him.

I look up. "No, I wouldn't be happy about that."

He holds my eyes. There's a weight in his gaze.

"Hey! Welcome back!"

A red-coated group clusters around Nico, the competing voices and bodies surrounding him in an instant. Hugo leaps over to the group, letting out an eager bark, and I'm alone in the sled.

These are the ski patrol volunteers, the people who make up Nico's community. They're laughing, and clapping him on the back, and wanting to hear all about his night stuck in the storm.

I look around, seeing the lodge in full swing. Cars are pulling into the lot, and families are checking in. It's suddenly all far too much.

"Wren?"

I turn my head toward Nico. He's at the center of the group, exactly where he belongs, and looking straight at me.

He's happy here. It's what he deserves.

"I'm going to head inside," I say, awkwardly clambering to my feet and climbing out of the sled.

"Can I come find you in a few minutes?"

He's so hopeful and open. So different from me.

I swallow so hard it hurts. "I don't think that's a good idea."

I can't turn away as his eyes shutter. "Yeah. Okay. Fine. Goodbye, Wren."

Goodbye, Nico.

M Y ROOM AT THE lodge, high on the topmost floor of the tower, is cozy and welcoming. I would even call it cute, but in a way that I can tolerate.

I've confirmed the thermostat is working, and the bed is plush and cozy, but as hard as I try, I just can't get warm.

I left Nico, and he left the lodge, a few hours ago. Now, my phone is charged, the swelling in my ankle has gone down after ice and elevation, and I'm jumping out of my skin.

I miss the sawing sounds of Hugo's snores, the assured press of Nico's fingers on my wrist, the comforting warmth of his front pressed to my back. This mattress might be top of the line, but an old cot in a messy cabin is the only thing on my mind.

Throwing the thick quilt off my lap, I grab my phone and make my way down the carpeted hallway.

The elevator is slow, filling with more and more people as I make my way down to the lobby. A small girl chatters to her parents about how she can't wait for her first lesson on the slopes. I relax into the sound of her voice and her mother's encouraging responses.

Maybe it isn't so bad here, after all.

We spill into the lobby, and I'm grateful to see there are two empty chairs near the great stone fireplace that is the centerpiece of the room. I walk over, still babying my ankle, and sink into one of the seats.

I don't know how long I'm there, but after a while, the front desk person is shooting me strange looks. I can't quite decipher whether she is worried *about* me or *because* of me. She's got short, spiky hair that's dyed the brightest green color I have ever seen. She would probably love my ski pants.

No one has dared to sit in the chair next to me, like I'm giving off some sort of sad-girl pheromones.

My skin itches. I crane my neck around as I hear the double doors at the front of the lodge open.

It's a family of four, laughing and lovely, but they are not the ones I want to see.

I want to see a dark, wavy head of hair. I want to see broad shoulders and teasing eyes that hide a deep vein of seriousness. I want to see a mess of brown, tan, and white fur, and droopy jowls, and dog drool.

I shoot out of my chair, nearly sending the furniture tipping back onto the floor.

The green-haired woman at the desk is staring at me, her finger poised on an intercom.

"I'm fine," I say, going for reassurance as I make my way toward her.

"I'm not so sure about that," she replies.

I inch closer, lurching for the edge of the check-in desk to relieve the pressure on my ankle. I can already feel it swelling up in anger again.

"You're Shan!" I yell as I catch sight of her name tag.

"Yes...I am..."

"You work at the front desk too? I thought you were in dispatch."

She's pressing a button on a phone keypad, and I'm sure it's only a matter of time before I'm asked to leave.

"This is getting really weird, lady. How—"

"I need you to find Nico for me!"

"Nico? What? Why?"

"It doesn't matter why. I just need to talk to him."

"He's not on patrol today."

"Can you give me his phone number, then?"

She crosses her arms over her chest, across the dark-green fleece with the Holly Peak logo on the left breast. "I'm not giving his phone number to a crazy person in the middle of the lobby."

"*Please,* Shan. I have to talk to him. I can't let him think that I—that I—"

She uncrosses her arms, and a slight dimple appears in one of her cheeks, like she's *enjoying* torturing me.

She leans in close, her voice barely above a whisper. "Can't let him think what?"

"That I don't love him! I have to tell him that I love him. Again. Still. Always."

She steps back, no longer hiding the full grin on her face.

"Tell him yourself."

I spin around, and he's there, Hugo leashed at his side.

I take two halting steps toward him before he's gathering me in his arms.

"Why aren't you resting?" he demands, keeping a firm hold on my elbows.

"I had to find you. To tell you—"

"You need to get off your feet. Now."

My world goes topsy-turvy when he scoops me up, tossing me over his shoulder in a fireman's carry.

"This is very undignified," I say, my breath coming fast as my stomach bobs against his shoulder.

"Don't care," he says, walking with practiced ease to the elevators. Hugo streams around his legs.

I peek up to see Shan and a bunch of other lodge guests grinning. One guy even claps. It's embarrassing, but also kind of sweet.

When we reach the elevator, Nico sets me down. I'm panting, though he is the one who was just lugging me around.

"What floor?"

"Six."

I open my mouth, uncertain if he heard my confession to Shan.

He presses a single finger to my lips as the elevator dings. A moment later, I'm airborne again, accepting my fate with an eye-roll.

"You could let me walk, you know. It isn't that far to the room."

"Not happening. I shouldn't have walked away from you this morning in the first place. I should have done this the minute we got to the lodge. Room key, please."

I sigh heavily. "It's in my back pocket."

I allow him to fetch the key and open the door. Once inside, he tosses me gently onto the bed. Hugo hops up, burrowing into the tousled quilt.

Nico kneels at the foot of the bed, undoing the laces of my shoes as I sit and stare at the top of his head.

"Swelling has gone down."

"Yep."

"Got enough ice for it?"

"I have a little more in the ice bucket. The machine is close."

"Good, good."

"Nico, what are we—"

"Did you mean it, Wren?"

"Mean what?"

"What you told Shan downstairs."

So, he did hear me. I'm not sure whether to be embarrassed or happy that the hardest part of my confession is out of the way. But he came back, and he whisked me away to my room, and he is *here*. Surely that means something.

"Every word," I say.

He grasps my hands in his, squeezing tight. "I realized not long after I left this morning that it was probably overwhelming for you when we got back. I should have recognized that, gone slower, not taken it so personally that you weren't ready for another serious talk."

"Nico, it's okay. I got scared, and I retreated again, after I promised I wouldn't do that."

"No, Wren. Retreat is one thing. You can retreat when you need to. I'll be here, waiting for my next chance with you. It's the thought of you disappearing, surrendering that I can't stand."

I raise a shaking hand to his cheek. "I didn't disappear. I was coming to find you. No more waiting. Not for either of us."

"I missed you so much, Wren."

"I missed you too. These last few hours have been..."

"I know." He tips forward, resting his forehead on my shoulder. "Will you stay?"

We're going to need to come up with a plan, figure out the logistics of moving the contents of my storage unit to Holly Hill. I'll need to decide what I'm doing for the rest of my life. Find a job. But doing life with Nico sounds better than doing anything apart from him.

"I'll stay."

He picks his head up, his brown eyes wet. "Wren. I love you too. Now. Still. Always."

I smile, letting the perfect peace I'm feeling shine through. "Want to give me a tour of my new home?"

"Absolutely."

CHAPTER THIRTEEN

Nico

HUGO AND I JOG up the three steps of my porch, and I shove open the hunter-green front door to my townhouse.

"We're back!" I juggle two fresh dirty chai lattes as I unhook Hugo's leash and hang it on the metal hook on the wall.

Wren looks up from the couch when I walk into the living room. Her legs are outstretched, and I see the neon blue of an ice pack on her injured ankle. She hits me with her rare soft smile, and I pause.

Wren is here, in my house, on my couch, looking like she's right where she belongs. I know it's where she is meant to be, and I hope she feels the same way.

We didn't get very far on our tour of Holly Hill. We'd gotten a little sidetracked, first in her room where I made her come with my fingers and then my mouth. Then, she'd asked to see my house, where she promptly decided my dark-gray sectional couch—the one that takes up nearly the entirety of the tiny space—was her new favorite spot.

I'd run out to Snowcap Café to grab our drinks. The place had been busy, what with people in town desperate for a caffeine fix after being trapped in their houses during the travel ban. Alice had looked unusually glum, but I figured it was just the stress of the snowstorm and the subsequent crowd.

"Hi," Wren says, wiggling her toes.

"Hi," I say, stalking over to her to lay a firm kiss on her lips.

"Hmm," she says in a moan.

The base of my spine tingles when her tongue touches mine.

"We'll never get around to that tour of Holly Hill if you keep that up," I say as I pull away.

She grins wryly. "I'll have plenty of time to see the town—since I'll be living here and all."

"You were serious about that? You really want to move to Holly Hill?"

She sobers. "I meant it, Nico. I want to live here and be with you. I don't think it will be easy. I've been all over the country for almost a year, and before that, my life was all about taking care of Dad. But this thing with Dad's ashes was good for me. My grief support group is helping. It will be an adjustment, but I think I can do it. Spending time around you and Hugo, meeting people like Shan, has helped me realize that I do need connections. I can't live my life numb anymore."

"You don't think you'll get sick of it? Staying in one place?"

She shakes her head. "I stayed in one place for years. These last few months were an anomaly."

"My place is small. I wasn't planning on moving anytime soon." That's an understatement. I bought the townhouse two years ago after scrimping and saving. The two-bedroom is enough for me and Hugo, but will it be enough for Wren?

"Your house is adorable."

"I don't have a garage."

She shrugs. "Dad always had so much shit in our garage that I could never park my car there. I'm used to it."

"The kitchen is tiny. I don't even have a dishwasher."

"You also have a wood-burning stove in the living room, tons of built-in cabinets, and a yard with trees. Not to mention, you live less than five minutes from a ski resort. I've been living in my *car*. What's this really about, Nico?"

"I just want this all to be perfect for you. So you'll never want to leave."

She surprises me with a full-blown laugh then sits up fully. I'm careful of her ankle as she shifts around until we are sitting side by side. She takes my hand firmly in hers. "When I left before, it wasn't about stuff, or where we lived, or anything like that. It was because..."

"Because you knew you couldn't rely on me to support you back then. Not with how I was behaving and what you had to manage for your dad." I'd known it without her even saying it outright.

"Partly, yes. But you're not that guy anymore, are you?"

She says it like a question she already knows the answer to. Like she knows that I'm the one who needs it.

"Not always. But I'd say tossing you over my shoulder this morning was a decidedly *Dom* type of recklessness." I'll never be totally divorced from that side of my personality.

"I love that part of you too. That's the part that had you skiing down a mountain in the middle of a snowstorm to rescue me. You're just a little more cautious about it now."

She's right, I realize. Hugo licks our joined hands, and the last vestige of insecurity washes away. It will resurface, I'm sure, but Wren and I will muddle through. Together.

Wren scoots over to allow Hugo to nose further into our space. I'm being displaced by my dog...again. Despite my envy, I scratch the top of his head just the same.

Wren looks up at me, her face serious again. "I need you to know that my disappearing before wasn't totally about you and your reliability. You've *always* been the guy you are now too. I was so afraid of having a hard conversation that I decided to run away instead. After that, I was too embarrassed and too overwhelmed with being a caregiver that I kept myself closed off from even thinking about reconnecting with you or our other friends. That's a tendency I'm still trying to overcome."

It's my turn to reassure her in this back and forth that I hope is never-ending. "You're having the hard conversation right now."

Wren Dunbar doesn't preen—ever—but she does something fairly close to it while sitting in my living room. "I am, aren't I?"

"Without a doubt."

"If we're all done with the heavy talk, can I ask you something?"

"Of course."

"I know I can't get back on the trails until this thing heals." She flicks her eyes down to her ankle.

"Two to four weeks at most. We'll get you out there before the season ends, I promise."

"Good, good," she says with twin nods. "But...do you think I'd be decent at, say, your job?"

I tilt my head. "Ski patrol?"

"Yeah. I mean, I don't have any formal medical or first-responder training, but when I took care of Dad, I got pretty comfortable with basic medical stuff. It doesn't scare me. Plus, there's that job opening at Holly Peak..."

"It's more than just skiing. You'd have to get certified...either EMT or the Outdoor Emergency Care training program through National Ski Patrol."

Her throat bobs, her first sign of uncertainty since I walked in. "Do you think I'll be able to handle the coursework. I haven't been in school for a while..."

I smash my lips down onto hers. "Wren, you're the most brilliant woman I've ever met. Come to work with me, see what a full day looks like—minus the blizzard—and we'll talk more. I don't want you jumping into something because of me. You need to love it for you."

Her head bobs excitedly. "How about tomorrow?"

"You won't be able to ski yet with your ankle. And it will be a lot of sitting around until you're healed up."

"What if I hang out with Shan in dispatch?"

I groan. Just what I need, the two of them getting up to no good. "She'll talk your ear off—probably about me."

"I am going to eat up Nico stories like you would not believe. I missed nine years with you. I'm on a crash course to learn everything about you."

"Good thing we have the rest of our lives for that, huh?"

Her wide smile shimmers with the snow-bright light of our second chance.

Epilogue

WREN

THE OFF-SEASON

"Last tuition check is sent," I say, spinning around in the wonky desk chair.

It's the same chair Nico sat in when we were stranded here last winter in this same cabin.

He's sitting on top of the exam table, which he just finished clearing off and wiping down.

We like to come out here every so often, not to spend the night but to tidy up together and reminisce about the wild experience that brought us back to one another. During the ski season, it was one of the few places we could escape to, away from the prying eyes and ears of the ragtag group of volunteer patrollers who tend to follow Nico around.

I can't say I blame them. He is pretty damn wonderful, and I don't even like most people.

"Did you get class with the instructor you wanted?"

I twist my lips. "Nope. It was full. I had to enroll in the session with Cartwright."

Nico gives me a rueful grin. "Sorry, babe. I know he wasn't your favorite during the spring semester."

"He gives terrible feedback. How am I supposed to be a good EMT when the dude teaching me just says, *'Not like that,'* but refuses to tell me how to do it instead?"

"You could always transfer into another class."

"Yeah, but he's the only option for the summer session, and I really want to get this course finished so I can sit for the exam. I'm getting sick of driving into Merlin Heights every week for class."

He shakes his head at me before hopping down from the exam table and sauntering over. He takes my face between both his hands and gives me that telltale smirk of his.

"Guess I'll just have to find some way to make your nights better on..."—he glances over my shoulder to the computer screen that still has my course schedule displayed—"Mondays, Wednesdays, and Fridays."

I tilt my face up to receive his kiss as I wrap my fingers around his wrists. Only Nico could make me look forward to attending class with the instructor from hell.

Alright, he's not the worst teacher in the world, but my tolerance for bullshit is at an all-time low. I'm ready for fieldwork and to take the national exam to become an EMT, and I'm tired of waiting. Nico put me through the paces last season once my ankle healed. I was able to ski every run at Holly Peak within a few weeks. After that, I sweet-talked him into letting me practice with the toboggan. I'm good, perhaps even better than Nico, at the skiing part of things.

It's the classroom stuff that I want to get out of the way. Nico insists that I'll be fine, and he's been helping me study every weekend.

I'm grateful that he has the time to help me. The off-seasons are slower for him, though he still has responsibilities at the resort. But it's been relaxed enough that we took a week-long trip to Rocky Mountain National Park with Hugo. I even mustered up the courage to see some of my old friends from college. It was awkward at first, but like Nico, they'd understood once I took the time to explain what happened and where I'd been. I doubt we'll be lasting friends again, but we won't be strangers anymore, and that's a start.

Now, I've been finding my place in Holly Hill. I take Hugo on daily walks to Snowcap Café, where Alice is determined to turn me into her new best friend so that Nico and I can go on double dates with her and her very nice, very uptight boyfriend.

The thought of going on a double date makes me want to vomit, so I'm lucky that my coursework keeps me busy enough that I have a valid excuse.

I have made one almost-friend named Juniper. She's constantly traveling, a boon for someone like me, who needs to ease into friendship one pointed toe at a time.

Shan, of course, has been the exception. We took to one another almost as quickly as Nico and I did when we first met as teenagers.

I'm still going to my online grief support meetings with Marcqui. Hugo is a hit whenever he intrudes on screen.

I'm getting there, finding little ways to branch out and connect with life again. To connect with who I am and who I used to be. To work toward who I want to be going forward.

"Come on, let's get out of here. It's way too hot in this place."

I breathe into Nico, going boneless as he lifts me out of the chair and into his arms.

He hasn't let go of the habit for some reason. He says he likes the weight of me, likes how he always knows where I am when he's got his arms wrapped around me.

I like it too.

The ground outside the cabin crunches beneath Nico's feet. It's been a dry summer, and the peak is desperate for rain.

Hugo sprints over to us with a happy bark. Nico is still his favorite person, but I'm a very close second.

"Hey, big guy," I say as Hugo jumps at my dangling legs. "Think you can put me down now?" I ask Nico.

"I guess," he grumbles but slowly lowers me down from the bridal carry.

As soon as my feet hit dirt, I slip my arms around him, resting my head on the soft fabric of his worn green t-shirt. No matter how much I love living in Holly Hill, it doesn't beat this feeling. Nico is my home wherever we are.

He runs a hand over the top of my head, twisting his fingers in my ponytail. "Ready to hike back?" he asks.

I nod.

"Want to take the trail where your dad is?"

There's a lump in my throat. It will probably always be there. I nod into Nico's chest, giving him one last squeeze in thanks for never forgetting my father and the reason we found each other again.

I look back at our nondescript cabin. "This place is pretty great, you know?"

Nico gives me a small smile, knowing exactly what I'm getting at. "Someday soon, we'll come back here. Maybe that's where you'll agree to marry me."

I raise my brows. "Oh, really? You're so confident I'll say yes?"

"Ninety-nine percent sure. So long as I don't find any Scooby Doo stationery laying around the house, I think I'm good."

"I don't want a big wedding."

"Oh, I know. Justice of the Peace with only the necessary witnesses in attendance."

I let out a soft laugh through my nose. He knows me well. Now, still, and always.

"You're a nut," I tell him.

He just shakes his head, taking my hand between his as we start our descent down the trail. "The fact that you're already planning our wedding just tipped me over to one-hundred percent certainty."

"You've never lacked for confidence."

"Only with you."

"Not anymore, though, right?"

"Not anymore," he says firmly.

"Let's go home, Nico."

Hugo lets out a jubilant woof as the three of us make our way down the trail, aiming for home.

Acknowledgements

First, thank you to all the readers who made it here! Whether this is the first book of mine that you've read, or the third, I appreciate you taking a chance on a new indie author.

To my husband and two wonderful children. You give my life meaning.

To Jennifer and Harriet. Remember when these books were crazy ideas on a spreadsheet?! We are making our dreams come true and I could not be more proud of us.

To Jenn for your constant kindness and consistent edits. Maybe one day I will know the difference between further and farther.

To Yen for absolutely NAILING Nico, Wren, and Hugo on this cover. Your talent is going to take you far! Ευχαριστώ.

To Alyssa for your lovely map and illustrations.

Finally, I want to acknowledge my beautiful sister-in-law, Michelle, who passed away while I was drafting this novella. If you feel compelled, please consider donating to the National Brain Tumor Society and ACCT Philly, the organization where Michelle adopted her first love, a dog named Harry.

Read All of the Holly Hill Winter Novella Collection!

Also by Rachel Kaye

About the Author

Rachel writes small-town romantic comedies with plenty of steam and twice the heart. She is a reader first, writer second, and holds the principle of happily ever after as sacred. Rachel lives in Western New York with her bearded husband, two rambunctious children, a snuggly cat, and a one-eyed Chihuahua.

Rachel is co-founder of Book & Brew Creative LLC, alongside fellow authors Jennifer Aline and Harriet Banter.